The Voyage of The Arctic Tern

Hugh Montgomery was born and brought up in Plymouth and has always had a love of the sea. A keen diver, he spent much of his youth on or under the waves and was part of the team that salvaged Henry VIII's flagship, the Mary Rose. He began writing The Voyage of The Arctic Tern as a Christmas present for his godchildren, but didn't finish it until three years later! He decided to publish the book himself — with great success, winning Book of the Year and Poetry Book of the Year at the David St John Thomas Charitable Trust Self-publishing Awards 2000. Leader of the group of researchers who discovered the first "gene for human fitness" in 1998, Hugh works as a consultant in intensive care at University College London. He loves deep-sea diving and mountaineering.

Nick Poullis is a painter and artist whose work has been displayed in many private exhibitions and galleries both in the UK and abroad, winning several prizes and awards. Born and brought up in Amersham, Buckinghamshire, Nick now lives in the Mayenne region of France.

This book is for those rare people who inspire one to
go further, and permit one to try. Especially to Eric
Neale, my parents, and of course Mary...
HM

For Marion
NP

First published by
Walker Books Ltd 2002
87 Vauxhall Walk, London SE11 5HJ

This edition published 2003

2 4 6 8 10 9 7 5 3 1

Text © 2000, 2002, 2003 Hugh Montgomery
Illustrations © 2000 Nick Poullis
Cover illustration © 2002 Gary Blythe

The right of Hugh Montgomery and Nick Poullis respectively to be identified as author
and illustrator of this work has been asserted by them in accordance with the Copyright,
Designs and Patents Act 1988

This book has been typeset in Weiss and Centaur
Lettering by Jovica Veljovic

Printed and bound in Great Britain by Creative Print and Design (Wales), Ebbw Vale

British Library Cataloguing in Publication Data:
a catalogue record for this book is available
from the British Library

ISBN 0-7445-9483-9

www.walkerbooks.co.uk

The Voyage of The Arctic Tern

Hugh Montgomery

Illustrated by Nick Poullis

WALKER BOOKS
AND SUBSIDIARIES
LONDON · BOSTON · SYDNEY

Foreword

Sometimes the unexpected happens, and in the modern world, in which the exciting years of childhood seem to be dominated by computer games, a new book arrives which delights the heart and the mind.

The Voyage of The Arctic Tern *is an epic tale of sailing ships and sailors. It bristles with avarice, sunken treasure and treachery, but good men triumph and bad men are exposed as base and worthless. Tales like this occur throughout history and they have been told over the centuries in many languages and by people of very different backgrounds. It is the author's use of lyrical verse to tell the tale three ways at three different periods of our maritime history that sets this book apart.*

This beautiful, descriptive narrative and the outstanding illustrations by Nick Poullis open the imagination and bring back memories to those of us who use the sea as our workshop. I hope it will encourage many young readers to understand and love the sea and sailing ships. Then perhaps they will dream a few dreams and, like the author, go on to explore the wonderful world beneath the sea for themselves.

Mrs Margaret Rule, CBE, FSA

BOOK ONE

The Present Day

PLYMOUTH

IN England lies the naval town of Plymouth,
The home of submarines and ships of war,
Of frigates, battleships and pleasure cruisers,
Of ferries, cargo boats and many more.
In summer, tourists throng along the seafront
Or splash along the beach at Bovisand
Or climb the *Mayflower* steps where Pilgrim Fathers
Sailed to colonize a distant land.

But when you visit, try to look about you,
Beyond the souvenirs and pleasure trips:
Imagine what this place might once have looked like
When Plymouth Sound was full of wooden ships.
The ancient port would be full of dangers:
Of vagabonds and smugglers – pirates too –
And simply walking out alone one evening
Could find you coming round as press-ganged crew.

When there, perhaps you'll chat to some old sailor –
A wise man who can tell you all the tales
Of local crooks and privateers and pirates:
The gold and silver carried as they sailed.
Perhaps he'll speak of caves crammed full with diamonds,
Of treasure chests long buried out of reach,
Of times when customs men and smugglers battled
And pearls and blood were spilled at Wembury beach.

But there's one tale I know that he won't mention:
Of Bruno and his quest for Spanish gold.
And of the little boat which he then captained
I guarantee you'll never hear a word.
Things happen here in Plymouth in the winter,
And of such things you'd surely never learn.
So take your seat and listen while I tell you
Of Bruno and his ship, *The Arctic Tern…*

TALES OF A WINTER'S NIGHT

NOW once a year (one special night
As orange moonlight seeps through cracks
In clouds which wander wintry skies
Past splintered stars all set in black),
A freezing fog engulfs the town –
Quite where it comes from no one knows,
But somewhere out in Plymouth Sound
It bubbles from the sea, and grows.

Most sailors won't put out at all
Preferring, if they can, to stay
At home, or else in foreign parts,
Each year upon this special day.
But those who have been on the sea
And witnessed it, most often say
That they first sight this eerie fog
Near Renne's Rocks in Heybrook Bay.

It swirls across the silent sea,
Milk spilled on inky ocean's floor.
In half an hour, or maybe less,
It's crossed the Sound and reached the shore.
And to the Barbican it comes:
The temperature begins to fall
As tongues of mist lick seafront stones,
Spill clammy dribbles o'er the wall.

And rising up, great rolling banks
Will spill and tumble, start to set.
Pale haloes form around the lights
And cobbles bathe in ice-cold sweat.
On silence, muffled sounds intrude –
The creak of timbers. Bilge's slop.
The lonely whale-song of foghorns.
Licking water's slap and drop.

And from the mist appear twelve ships
Each sailing in the wake before.
They make their way to Sutton Pool
Then moor to rings upon the shore.
And from each boat, a fisherman
Steps out and walks along the side
And makes his way across the front.
Seeks the Admiral MacBride.

The pub itself is quite deserted.
No one comes to drink this night
Nor dares to walk the cobbled streets –
And no one will until first light.
The doors will all be locked securely –
Shutters up, all curtains drawn,
All children banished to their beds
Where each shall stay until the dawn.

Inside the pub a table stands
With thirteen places, thirteen chairs.
And by each seat a place is set
And at each place, some food prepared.
Each has an ancient china plate
And each a frothing pint of beer
And on each plate some black rye-bread –
The meal identical each year.

These twelve men take their silent places,
Rise as one and turn to face
The empty chair which heads the table;
One man missing from his place.
Now solemnly they take their drinks
In foreign tongue they make a toast
Raise glasses to an absent friend:
"The memory of Bruno's ghost!"

For some time thence they sit and talk
Of fearsome days and nights long past,
Of howling winds and heaving seas
And days of toil beneath the mast.
And by tradition, tell the story
(One of which you soon will learn)
Of treason, treachery and treasure:
The voyages of *The Arctic Tern*.

They leave the building some time later,
Bolt the door and turn the key,
Retrace their steps and board their boats
Then silently slip out to sea.
Behind, they leave the room deserted –
Bruno's table place still set.
His chair still drawn. Plate undisturbed.
His bread and beer untouched. As yet.

THE NEXT MORNING

NOW in the morning, those that come
Will find those battered trawlers gone.
The fog will clear, the frost will melt,
And all that aching tension felt
Throughout the night and recent days
Will dissipate just as the haze.
Doors and curtains open wide
In houses by the waterside
And fisher folk will meet and greet
And chatter on the cobbled streets,
Relieved to shed that nameless fear
Until the winter of next year.

As early sunrays seek the frames
And push their way through grimy panes,
So bars and bands and chinks of light
Pick out the places where last night
Those dozen sailors met to toast
The memory of Bruno's ghost.
And as they pierce the dusty air
The rays light up that thirteenth chair.

But all is not as it had been –
Quite different is the morning scene.
Consumed is Bruno's fine repast:
A foam of ale runs down the glass.
The meal has gone. All that remains
Are crumbs. A crust. A beer-glass stain.

Seen trailing from the bolted door
Wet footprints mark the oaken floor.
They lead directly to the chair.
Some salt and sand collected there
Suggest perhaps he sat awhile
To eat the bread and sup his ale.
From there the prints, seen clearly still,
Have made their way towards the till
Upon the top of which is left
A token for his beer and rest:
Upon an ancient china plate
A Spanish silver piece of eight.

The barman – you will learn his name –
For many years has been the same.
How long this is, no one seems sure –
But must be thirty years or more.
This fellow, later in the day,
Collects that silver – not as pay,
But places it behind the bar
Inside an ancient stoneware jar,
Wherein it joins some thirty more,
Collected over years before.

Should someone suffer failing health
Or lose their sight, or lose their wealth;
Lose self-esteem, their will to live,
Feel life has nothing left to give,
Then maybe they'll suppress their pride,
Seek out the Admiral MacBride
And leave a note pinned on the door
– So plead the weak, the sick, the poor.
And to those souls, or so they say,
Will come a silver coin that day
Each taken from inside that jar
Which lies, in turn, behind that bar.

But oh, what mystery! Is this
Some endless source of happiness?
For though the jar will oft bring cheer,
Throughout the seasons, year on year,
The level in the jar won't fall –
In fact, it never drops at all.

To understand such acts as these
You have to cross time's stormy seas
To meet with pirates, kings and ghosts,
Find treasure sunk off England's coast.
Cast loose your moorings. Set your sails.
Let mind's strange winds and tides prevail
And, shortly, in Seville you'll land
Where treachery is close at hand…

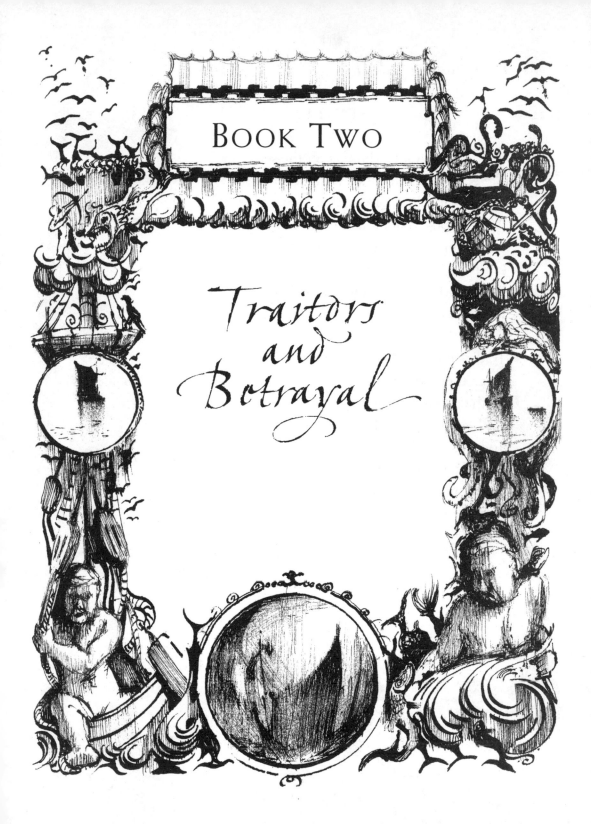

BOOK TWO

Traitors
and
Betrayal

1 Spain and the Spanish King

SEVILLE

SUNLIGHT shatters off the sea
And warm winds waft around a host
Of palms, caressed by gentle breath,
Which nod, content, along the coast.
Tangy smells of Spanish orange
Lift from fruit trees just inland
Which drift and shimmer in the heat
As if afloat on seas of sand.

Traders on Seville's old seafront
Stack their stalls with scents and spice,
With crafted gold or silk in rolls,
And as they work, they shout their price.
Today is just like any day
For traders come to sell or buy.
But in the castle on the hill
Another picture meets the eye.

The servants in the castle weep.
No brightly coloured flags are flown.
The sentries stoop and shake their heads.
The gates are locked. Portcullis down.
For though the walls are eight feet thick
And carved in blocks of solid stone
Still death has made its way inside
And stalked their king upon his throne.

They loved their king. It hurt them so
To see him suffer in this way.
It seemed they'd need a miracle
Were he to last another day.
How could they know that fighting death
He stood, alone, no chance to win?
For none of them had recognized
The enemy who lurked within.

In life we find two groups of men:
Some dare not trust, try to defend
Themselves from everyone they meet –
See enemies in all their friends.
The other group are noble sorts –
Seek good in everyone they see.
Their trusting nature often leads
To dangerous gullibility.

Now on the whole, there's little doubt
Contentment comes to those who live
An honest life without mistrust,
Who rarely take, but often give.
But oh! The pain which comes to them
When friends are enemies disguised.
With trust betrayed, and no defence,
They risk their all, may lose their lives.

And so it was that servants wept
To see their king draw failing breath
As treason's unseen smothering hands
Clung on to cause now certain death.
But often fate will intervene
To damn the wrong, support the right,
Protect the righteous even when
It seems that they have lost the fight.

MORGAN

A RICH man called Morgan was known to the people
But views of him differed with whom you might ask.
Both nobles and courtiers thought of him highly
(Opinions coloured by "gifts" in oak casks).
But ask those who laboured all day on the sea
What they thought of the man, and of what else they'd learned,
And they'd tell of a smuggler, a killer and cheat,
Whose nickname of "Mad Dog" was truly well earned.

He owned half Seville, and a fleet of old ships
Which he used for importing his silver and gold.
But mixed with the jewellery (whose carriage was legal)
Were other more lucrative cargoes he sold.
He smuggled all manner of drink and tobacco
Defending this trade with an uncontrolled wrath.
Should anyone else dare compete in such deals
Well – he'd not stop at killing such men in his path.

On land he was dressed in a way almost formal.
At sea he'd discard all this fashion and charm –
Wear a blue pirate's tunic and razor-sharp cutlass;
With gold braid and tassels stitched onto each arm.
His herald (embroidered in gold on the pockets
And also on pennants he raised to the skies)
Spoke of stealth and of strength and of far-reaching powers:
'Twas an octopus glaring with fiery red eyes.

For his sport, he would sail down the coast for a day
And would climb to the crow's nest, and there he would stand
With his telescope, scanning the distant horizon
And searching the inlets and bays of the land.
When he sighted a ship, he would swing to the helm
And would head for that vessel and shout to the crew
Who would take down the fiery-eyed octopus emblem:
A black skull and crossbones the flag they then flew.

Having seized all their cargo, he'd muster the men
And insist that they watch as their torched vessel sank.
Completing his pleasure, he'd keelhaul the captain
And make all the rest of the crew walk the plank.
There were thus no survivors to tarnish his image.
His closest of consorts would never suspect
That the "gentleman merchant" was really a thief
Who stood at the wheel on a pirate ship's deck.

But unknown to Morgan, there was one survivor –
An admiral, Hunter, who'd slipped from his grasp.
When he'd captured that ship, Morgan tied up the man
And then hurled him with glee from the top of the mast.
He never resurfaced, so Morgan assumed
That the fall must have stunned him and caused him to drown;
Whilst in fact far below Hunter fought himself free
Of the ropes and the sacking with which he was bound.

He had floated on currents for almost two days
(And from sunstroke and thirst might have easily died)
When a ship sailing past him caught sight of his body.
They lifted him carefully over the side.
The salt-crusted captain was kind to poor Hunter
Shared food and his clothing, went out of his way
To get him back home to his wife in north England –
A debt which Lord Hunter would one day repay.

THE SPANISH KING IN SEVILLE

THE king was a kind man, a fine man of honour
A man who would always try hard to do good.
He cared for the weak and supported the needy.
He sought to win friends and make peace if he could.
The people adored him, admired him and honoured him.
Merchants lived happily, safe and secure
Giving part of their earnings in tax as he asked them,
Happy to see how he tended the poor.

But some men were greedy, despising the king
And resenting the taxes he put on their wealth;
Convinced they should fight and in war win more riches
And spend not one coin on the sick or their health.
Morgan was one man of such a persuasion:
Begrudging each dollar of tax that was spent.
He was shrewd though, pretending to honour the king,
Who thus never suspected his deep discontent.

As time passed this loathing became an obsession.
With friends, who would never report what he said,
He would mutter and curse, say they'd all do much better
If sickness should strike and the king end up dead!
Consumed with such bitterness, Morgan thus plotted:
He'd work for the poor, make his loyalty known.
But once in a post above any suspicion
He'd poison the king and himself take the throne.

In only a year he'd become Chief Adviser.
His views on all matters were frequently sought.
The king came to value his judgement most highly.
He soon was in favour with all in the court.
He tended the servants and treated them kindly:
He increased their wages and won them as friends.
In fact, he considered this "low life" quite worthless –
Control of the court was a means to an end.

Each morning, the personal cook to the king
Would rise early and make his way down to the shore
Where he'd purchase the best of the fish and the produce
And carry it back to the kitchen and store.
It was therefore most odd when the cook left one morning
And did not return by the end of the day.
It would seem he must have run off with the money
(At least, that's what Morgan was soon heard to say).

It was now Morgan's job to employ a new cook
Which he did that same day – found a man who'd do fine.
At the time no one questioned quite where he had come from
Nor why he should bring a supply of sweet wine.
But a man who had lived through the pirate attacks
Would remember the faces of all of that crew
And would tell you that Morgan's new cook for the king
Had in fact been the cook on his pirate ship too.

A little while later, the king became ill.
He grew sicker and weaker with each passing day,
And with headaches and cramps, he'd eat scarcely a morsel –
It seemed to them all he would soon pass away.
A doctor was called, who declared himself baffled,
Unable to diagnose what had gone wrong.
With leeches and potions he hoped for a cure,
Though the king, he suspected, would not last for long.

As the illness progressed, it would often be noted
How Morgan would come, thinking nothing of time,
And sit by the bedside and tend him for hours;
Would moisten royal lips with that sweet-tasting wine.
The king was most grateful, astonished that Morgan
Should humble himself in the role of a nurse;
Found comfort in drinking the wine that he brought him
Though afterwards, sometimes, he'd feel strangely worse.

The monarch knew well that his life would soon end
And was keen that his heir should be heard as a voice
Of compassion, integrity, love and of honour.
His adviser was clearly the obvious choice.
The king called his council, announced his decision:
To Morgan, his friend and adviser, he'd hand
The burdens of ruling the whole Spanish Empire,
Of protecting both the rich and the poor in the land.

Just as Morgan had planned, then, events had unfolded:
The throne, he felt sure, would be his on that day.
He could not have foreseen, though, the card fate would deal him
By way of a boat which arrived in the bay.

2 *The English Queen and her Plan*

THE QUEEN AND LORD HUNTER

IN London, in that very year
(The day the cook had disappeared:
As Mad Dog Morgan sought to reign
By killing off the king of Spain)
The English queen called to her court
The counsellors and aides she thought
Might guide her as she tried to make
Her peace with other heads of state.

The English navy long had fought
To rule the waves, and each year sought
To help sustain her colonies,
Returning all their wealth by sea.
This violent conquest by the sword
Brought untold riches from abroad
With all the wealth of other lands
Delivered into English hands.

Few men, it seemed, would thus support
These plans for peace when they had brought
Vast wealth and booty – massive hoards
Of gold and silver – from abroad.
A change to peaceful policy
Could make these men sworn enemies.
So any such diplomacy
Would need the utmost secrecy.

So, to her court the queen now called
The man she trusted most of all.
From Durham, then, Lord Hunter came
To be her messenger to Spain.
Now admiral of all her fleet,
She knew that he would be discreet
And not reveal her secret plan
To any other Englishman.

She asked that he should seek a crew
Of men he trusted through and through
To never breathe a single word
To anyone of what they'd heard:
A crew who'd brave the stormy seas
And bear her message loyally.
To Spain would stretch an English hand
To offer peace between two lands.

Lord Hunter heard what she proposed
Then, without question, he arose.
He bowed, and swore an oath that he
Would bear her message faithfully.
He took the scroll which she proffered
And left the room without a word.
"Godspeed," she called, "and understand:
Our hopes of peace lie in your hands."

LOUISE AND LORD HUNTER

IN Durham, a woman was patiently waiting,
For Hunter had promised Louise he'd return.
He saddled his horse, and at once left to see her:
He'd given his word and would not let her down.
'Midst stormclouds and rain, then, he rode night and day
Until wet and bedraggled he came to her home.
She kissed him. At once, she could tell he was troubled
And asked if her father could leave them alone.

He knew time was short, that his life was at risk
From the perilous trip and the men he would cross.
In both Spain and England, some merchants made money
From warfare: to these, any peace would mean loss.
He'd promised the queen that he'd keep the plan secret:
That no one would hear what she'd asked him to do.
Louise, though, had promised she'd never betray him
And he, in his turn, had sworn honesty too.

He wept as he told her that now he must leave her;
He couldn't explain why or where he must go.
The chance he might die bore no terror at all:
The fact they were parting hurt more than she'd know.
He wished to make certain that, if fate decreed it
And death should befall him, the goods that he owned
Would be passed to the woman he loved above all:
That Louise would inherit his lands and his home.

Their marriage, he said, would bring strength to them both.
In spirit, they'd always be one from that day.
She'd know that his thoughts would be constantly with her
No matter how long he remained far away.
In practical terms, she would share his belongings,
Own half of his chattels and half of his land.
At least, should he die, he would know she'd be cared for.
He knelt as he begged her to offer her hand.

For a while she said nothing, but walked off alone
As she thought of his offer, and what she should do.
She knew she would love him wherever he went,
And she knew, to that love, she would ever be true.
This wedding day, then, would be what she had yearned for
She'd long dreamed of spending her life by his side;
But his leaving would make the day sad beyond measure.
She walked back to face him, and then she replied.

"I don't wish to know why it is you must leave me
Nor hear of the perils that threaten your life.
You know, though, I'll wait here until your return
And promise that then you shall make me your wife.
You'll not do so now, for the joy it would bring
Would be marred by the fact that we'd soon have to part.
Instead, let us wait for that day in the future
When marriage will mark not an end – but a start.

"Godspeed, then, my lord. May your journey be safe.
May you guard your own life as you'd surely guard mine.
Try to think of me daily at sunrise and sunset
For prayers shall I send you each day at those times.
Should you ever feel helpless, not know what to do,
Or are lonely or lost – when you feel you're alone –
Then just think of the strength which we have when together:
Its spirit will guide you and bring you back home."

He packed, then, in sorrow and left her next morning,
And rode off to Plymouth in search of a crew
And a ship that would carry him safely to Spain
And bring him back home to his native shores too.
Now only one man in the whole of the country
He trusted enough to enlist in this task:
'Twas the man who had once saved his life far away.
It was Bruno, the captain, he knew he must ask.

3 The Boat and Crew

THE ARCTIC TERN

STRANGE to tell, but no one knew just when the ship was made.
Her timbers, burned by sun and salt, seemed of a different age.
The old men claimed, as children, that they'd seen her,
and would tell
How every generation past remembered her as well.

They also noted, strangely, that she'd sailed through violent seas
But never once been seen to suffer any injury.
When howling storms had passed, they'd see her moored up by the wall;
With boats wrecked all around her, she'd bear not one scratch at all.

At forty feet, it seemed that she was far too small to brave
The minor coastal inlets, let alone vast ocean waves.
The ignorant dismissed her, for they never would have thought
That though she'd go to sea for months, she'd not once sail to port.

The clinker hull had darkened through the years of salty spray.
The wheel-house matched its colour, and the ageing sails were grey.
And if you looked quite closely, gazing up towards the prow,
A tiny bird with wings spread wide was painted on her bow.

Her name was carved upon a plaque of Scandinavian pine,
Though how it was she came by it was lost in mists of time.
But there above the rim of weed which grew beneath the tide,
Beside the bird, her name, *The Arctic Tern*, was seen inscribed.

Her captain also puzzled them: when questioned, they would frown
And say it seemed for ever that he'd lived here in the town.
He hadn't aged at all, they said, so far as they could see,
And generations past had seen him putting out to sea.

Remember how I told you that a pirate ship, one day
Had sunk a boat and drowned the crew in waters far away?
And how it was that Hunter had escaped the pirate grasp
And lived to tell the tale of how he'd tumbled from the mast?

Remember how he'd drifted, and how certain you can be
That he'd have died of thirst, or drowned, if not plucked from the sea?
Well, Bruno was that saviour who pulled him from the foam:
The Arctic Tern the vessel which then carried him back home.

Lord Hunter thus decided that to reach the Spanish port
He'd need to find a captain – it was Bruno whom he sought.
So now you know about her and can see her, bow to stern,
I'll tell you of the captain of that ship, *The Arctic Tern*.

BRUNO THE CAPTAIN

BRUNO was always a loner, they said,
But if sought he could often be found at low tide
In a Barbican pub he'd frequented for years –
Took its name from the admiral known as MacBride.
He would walk from his boat in his old leather boots,
And the barman would say that the man, without fail,
Would leave pools of salt water and sand from his feet
From the door to his seat in an unsightly trail.

A creature of habit, his meals were the same –
For his lunch and his supper, black rye-bread he ate.
A pint of best bitter would help him wash down
Every scrap, rind or crumb which still lay on his plate.
He would sit in the corner, and sipping his ale
He would nod to the barman as each pint was sent.
He'd say not a word, but would think private thoughts
And would watch as the fishermen came, drank and went.

All that he did, he would do the same way
Though the reason for this no one there could decide.
He would take off his jacket and, folding the sleeves,
He would lay it out flat on the floor by his side.
Whatever the size of the plate or the glass
He would empty them both, leaving nothing to show
For a whole loaf of bread or a bottle of rum;
He would finish each morsel before he would go.

His face had been tanned, such that no one could gauge
What his race or his natural colour had been,
While an old captain's cap (which he rarely removed)
Meant his hair – what was left of it – wasn't much seen.
A furrowed dark brow made him constantly thoughtful.
His eyes, though, were burning like fiery hot coals
So that those who by chance might have glanced at them briefly
Would feel that he'd glimpsed what lay deep in their souls.

A black tangled beard caked in decades of sea salt
Grew down from his chin in an unruly pile.
In the midst of this mass lay expressionless lips
The hair on his head was as thin as his smile.
But somehow one felt that this man was a friend:
That he'd help anyone whom he found in distress
And indeed, there were many who spoke of his acts
Of humility, sacrifice and of largesse.

Not many were counted as friends of Old Bruno.
Though those who had known him for years often tried
To engage him in talk of his life and adventures,
He'd never been known to respond or confide.
There *were* one or two, though, it seemed that he trusted;
With them he'd be seen to converse in hushed tones.
These men were the sort who could keep their own counsel –
Who didn't need company more than their own.

BRUNO'S FRIENDS:
ADRIAN THE BARMAN

THE first of these folk was the pub cook and barman.
Though many a customer liked a good chat,
These two seemed more earnest when talking together;
A bond seemed to bind them more deeply than that.
In fact, it was said by the elderly locals
That Adrian had in the past sailed as crew;
That *The Arctic Tern* left for those long months at sea
Not with Bruno alone, but with Adrian too.

A family man, he worked hard to support
A wife and two children, with each penny sent
Back to Bridget, his wife, and to sons Jack and Paddy
Who lived in his parents' home somewhere in Kent.
The pittance he kept was not spent on high living
But stored in a pot down below the oak bar
So his family, one day, could come down and live
In a house he would pay for with coins from the jar.

He cherished the hope that one day he might run
His own pub, where he'd serve not just beer but fine food.
The public would know what a great cook he was;
They'd hail him, and say to him, "Well, that *was* good!"
His customers teased him about his ambitions
And so did his friends. "I suspect," said his wife,
"That although in the future your dreams may come true,
We may well have to wait here until the next life!"

The reason she laughed at his plans for a business
Was clear, for each person who knew him agreed
That his heart was as big as the seas that he'd sailed,
And he'd always give money to those found in need.
In fact, those in trouble all knew what to do
And might secretly come to his doorway by night,
Leaving on it a note which would speak of their anguish.
Next day they'd find coins which would help ease their plight.

When Bruno was later requested by Hunter
To carry him safely to far Spanish shores
He looked for some crewmen to come on the voyage
And he thought of the men who'd gone with him before.
He thought, then, of Adrian. Bruno approached him
And asked him to pack and get ready to go.
As *The Arctic Tern* sailed, he'd be found in the galley
Preparing the food as the ship's cook below.

BRUNO'S FRIENDS:
THE DOCTOR

THERE was one more man who'd sailed with him before,
Who in years past had solemnly given his pledge
That with Bruno he'd travel again, should he ask;
A doctor of medicine, his name was Chris Edge.
He claimed that diseases were oft caused by creatures
Whose minuscule size made them hard to detect.
He was mocked – though his notes were one day read in France
By a fellow called Pasteur, who proved him correct.

His other great passion for things that were poisonous
Began in his childhood when, walking one day
He consumed some wild berries, and soon became ill
And was lucky that night he did not pass away.
He prided himself that there wasn't a man
Who knew more about toxins than he himself knew.
He'd tell at a glance if a man had been poisoned;
Say when it was done, and with what substance too.

He now lived in Oxford with Jenny his wife
Who had recently studied the silversmith's art.
The brooches and rings she now fashioned at home
Were much sought by the wealthy in near and far parts.
Her finest creation, in silver and gold,
Showed the heads of her daughters, with one on each side.
Victoria and Alexandra, together
Gazed out from a brooch which she wore with great pride.

So this was the man who, when summoned by Bruno,
Would hurry to Plymouth, avoiding delay,
To meet once again with his sailing companions
And hear what Lord Hunter himself had to say.
He knew that the trip would be one of importance:
A meeting was planned on which much was at stake.
His wife, from her dress, slipped the brooch that she wore
And passed it to Edge as a gift he could take.

4 The Departure

LORD HUNTER ARRIVES

THE long ride from Durham left Hunter exhausted,
But still he endeavoured, on reaching the port,
To seek his friend Bruno, who knew he was coming
(He'd first sent a message when at the queen's court).
He stabled his horse in a place close to Greenbank,
But first let it drink from a trough close to hand.
(If you walk there today you can find this same place
For the trough, carved in granite, is one that still stands.)

He walked down the hill and then on through a crossroads
Where now stands a church which was bombed in the war.
Then on to the seafront, across the stone cobbles
(The same ones you'll note that I've mentioned before).
Along the cold streets, past the rings to which vessels
Could tie themselves safely and lie until light
(The rings that I've mentioned, which twelve ghostly vessels
Would moor to, each year, on a cold winter's night).

He entered the pub, and at once saw his friend
Who was sitting, as normal, away from the door;
His jacket removed, with the sleeves neatly folded
Was laid out, by habit, beside on the floor.
How strange, though, that Bruno should seem to have known
Just precisely when Hunter would choose to arrive;
Not minutes before he had called to the barman
"A pint for my guest". It now stood to one side.

They sat there that evening and talked of old times,
Recollecting the details of just how, one day,
Lord Hunter was rescued from imminent death
By Bruno, whilst floating in seas far away.
It seemed, though, that Bruno would take little credit
For lifting him out, and for taking him home.
"Once I knew of your plight, could I ever have stayed?
If it wasn't for you, I would never have gone."

These words were surprising to Hunter, who'd thought
His discovery purely a matter of chance.
He'd believed that his rescue was not due to planning,
Owing nothing to choice, but to pure circumstance.
Besides, it defied any logic at all
To consider that Bruno could ever foretell
The events which befell him at Morgan's cruel hand,
To predict what would happen, and quite where as well.

Nonetheless, in the past he had had his suspicions.
In Plymouth, before, he had heard others talk
Of the strange way that Bruno would suddenly choose
To make ready his vessel and sail from the port;
How often such journeys would happen to take him
To places where others might suffer duress –
As if, so they said, he was doing a job
And was called to these missions by sensing distress.

It was midnight when all of the drinkers had gone
With Lord Hunter and Bruno the ones left behind.
Having served the last customer, Adrian joined them.
Together they shared in a jug of mulled wine.
They talked very little, content in the silence
Which only close friends ever share in this way
Leaving talk of their mission till Chris Edge arrived –
He would be there, most likely, within a few days.

By two in the morning, on reaching his lodgings,
Lord Hunter could finally fall into bed.
He'd rushed to the queen, to Louise then to Plymouth:
Completely exhausted, he slept like the dead.
His dreams were confusing, with pictures of Plymouth,
Of coastlines and palm trees and grapes on the vine;
And of pirates and kings, and an octopus glaring.
And also of bottles of sweet-tasting wine.

DOCTOR EDGE ARRIVES

HE woke the next morning to noise from the courtyard
A carriage, it seemed, had drawn up just outside.
From sounds that he heard and the things that were said,
It appeared that not long ago Edge had arrived.
So Lord Hunter arose and went out to the doctor
And greeted him warmly, explaining that he
Was the man who had asked for Old Bruno's assistance,
And one of the group who would soon put to sea.

They walked to the Barbican, went to the quay
Where the trawlers each morning unloaded, and where
Captain Jasper (a man now too old to set sail)
Cooked them fish, freshly caught, on a stall he had there.
Round the corner, at Jacka's, crisp loaves from the oven
Exuded sweet smells as they cooled on a tray.
Even now, Cap'n Jasper's still stands by the market;
The baker's shop, too, you can find to this day.

On the way back, they walked to the pub and left word
For the barman that Edge had now safely arrived.
Together they walked to their lodgings in Greenbank
Going up from the quay and along Bretonside.
The rest of the day they spent sorting possessions,
And packing those things which they'd load on the ship.
This was all done in secret, lest anyone learn
Of the voyage and reasons for making the trip.

MEETINGS

IN Greenbank, that evening, a carriage arrived
Bearing Adrian, Bruno, and one person more:
It was Daisy – a mongrel who lived on the boat,
And whose presence I ought to have mentioned before.
The doctor and barman were friends from past travels;
They'd both sailed with Bruno so now, at first sight,
Edge ran from the door to the side of the carriage
Whilst Adrian let out a whoop of delight.

The four of them now took their coach through the town.
They rode eastwards through Plymstock, and thus made their way
Past the clifftops at Staddon, and on up the hill
To descend, in the end, down to Bovisand Bay.
Far away from the town they were able to talk
Of their journey together without any fear
That by accident someone might catch what they said
(Or worse still, make deliberate efforts to hear).

They built a small hearth from some rocks which they gathered,
Lit dull sea-stained driftwood they found close at hand.
Young Adrian cooked them a meal in the embers
Which glowed like bright rubies in settings of sand.
When fine food and ale had been finished entirely
And flickering flames buttered gold on their cheeks,
The three who'd been summoned now sat in a circle
And looked to Lord Hunter, who started to speak.

He told them that decades of war had achieved
Very little but misery, hunger and pain;
That the queen wanted friendship, an end to the fighting,
And wished above all for a treaty with Spain.
To do this risked angering traders and merchants
Who'd profited, always, from war between lands;
She'd given Lord Hunter a personal message
Addressed to the king, to deliver by hand.

He said that the trip was most certainly dangerous,
And that Adrian ought to give thought to his sons,
For his death would leave Bridget alone with the children;
They'd all understand if he chose not to come.
And Edge should consider his wife and his children;
Should also take heed of the fact that his skills
Were important to all of the patients he treated.
He risked both his own life, and those of the ill.

The trip was a gamble. They might come away
With a treaty which guaranteed peace, on one hand.
On the other, the Spanish might think it a trap
And kill them, or jail them for years in their land.
Lord Hunter fell silent. The men, too, said nothing.
They thought of the mission which Hunter proposed
And balanced the good which might come to the country
With personal dangers. Then each man arose.

It was no great surprise to Lord Hunter to hear
That each one of them strongly approved of the plan
Whose success, they all felt, was of greater importance
Than dangers of any sort faced by one man.
The longer they waited, the greater the chance
That their presence was questioned, so any delay
Would be best kept as brief as it possibly could.
They agreed to be ready to sail in three days.

Three days later, they met in the pub close to midnight;
With everything packed, made their way to the ship.
Lost in thought, Bruno led them. Behind him went Adrian
Laden with foodstuffs they'd need for their trip.
Lord Hunter went next, with the scroll from the queen,
Next Daisy, tail wagging, who trotted beside.
Dr Edge (with his wife's silver brooch) boarded last.
On the deck, before sunrise, they ran with the tide.

5 The Voyage to Spain

THE VOYAGE BEGINS

IN such a way their voyage began.
The Arctic Tern seemed pleased once more
To butt her bows through choppy seas
And rush headlong from England's shore.
The path they took you still can see:
From Sutton Pool they travelled south,
Crossed peaty waters running east
In torrents from the Tamar's mouth.

Under Jennycliffe they sailed,
Around the point to Bovisand
And past the bay where, nights before,
They'd cooked their meal and made their plans.
Then out avoiding Renne's Rocks
(White water marked this sunken reef –
The Shagstone rising from its tip
Where many ships have come to grief).

A final sighting from the stars
And Bruno swung the helm around.
He set a course for Spanish sun
And left the curve of Plymouth Sound.
The boat rose on each heaving breaker,
Reached a crest, began to slide
Then launched itself towards the trough
And hurtled headlong down the side.

The heavy seas meant all the crew
Were working hard to tame the sails
And many were the times that waves
Would nearly wash them o'er the rails.
They never once, though, even thought
Of running from the howling storm
For Bruno, seeming undisturbed,
Exuded confidence and calm.

And sure enough, the winds died down;
The waves less high, their raging done.
Ahead, a sparkling orange path
Led onwards to a setting sun.
The breeze tugged gently at the lines
As Adrian prepared a meal.
They ate it seated at their posts,
With Bruno standing at the wheel.

That night, beneath a yellow moon,
They each told tales of voyages past
Of tidal waves, of wrecks and pirates,
Toil and sweat beneath the mast.
And so was passed the time on deck
Till finally, a silence fell
As each man turned expectantly
For Bruno to begin *his* tale…

BRUNO'S TALE

ONCE upon a time, he said,
At least a thousand years ago
Far to the north, there was a land
Of frozen rivers, ice and snow
Where in the winter bitter winds
Could even freeze the waves to glass
Whilst icebergs further out to sea
Would crush the boats which tried to pass.

As spring approached, the ice would melt
And soon bright flowers would surface where
Not long before, the ground lay hard;
Sweet scent would saturate the air.
The summer days were long and warm
And constant sunlight filled the skies
– Quite different from the winter, when
For months the sun would never rise.

And in those winter months, sometimes
Bright tongues of colour lit the night –
Kaleidoscopes of swirling flames
Which now we call the Northern Lights.
The rivers teemed with countless fish,
Wild geese and deer were often seen:
A place as close to paradise
As could exist outside one's dreams.

The population lived in huts,
And barns were built in which to smoke
The fish their men would catch at sea
And carry home to feed their folk.
These people were content to live
A simple life, would only seek
A shelter from the winter snows
And well-kept stores of fish to eat.

Now in a land not far from this
There lived a very different race.
They hunted, not for food to eat,
But merely to enjoy the chase.
Their life was one of ceaseless war;
They'd plunder all those parts around
Attacking with no cause at all,
Destroying anything they found.

Their leader was a hairy man
Who didn't speak so much as growl.
When happy, he would raise his head,
Stick out his lower jaw, and howl.
His upper jaw held two sharp teeth;
A leather collar round his throat
Was worn to match the name they gave him –
As was "Mad Dog's" wolfskin coat.

This tyrant wanted to destroy
The lovely land which I've described,
To crush the quiet villages,
Drive out the peaceful fishing tribes.
But just for fun, he thought he'd try
To bring the people to their knees
Without a fight. Could it be done?
He smiled. A plan had been conceived.

He'd send a ship to cruise the coast
And use some trickery, whereby
They'd board a local fishing boat
Whenever one was passing by
And once aboard, they'd offer jewels
To tempt the fisherman to sell
The very land in which he lived –
And all the villagers as well.

He chose the nastiest of men
And told them what they had to do.
They'd take a ship, then wait until
A fishing boat came into view.
They'd start a fire, then shout and scream,
And secretly they'd draw their swords;
The fisherman would come to help
And when he did, they'd leap aboard.

And so it was they stormed a boat
And pinned the captain to the deck;
Sweat soaked his beard and ran in rivers,
Stained the steel against his neck.
He said that he'd do anything
If only he'd be spared the blade.
Perhaps, they said, they'd let him go…
And in return suggest a trade?

He surely wasn't satisfied
To live a life as poor as this?
A man should seek some greater goal
If all he'd ever owned was fish!
A real man wouldn't be content –
Would happily sell all those fools
With whom he lived for something more…
Perhaps a bag of precious jewels?

With that, a bag of gems was brought
And tipped into his sweaty hand.
He gasped. The wealth now in his palm
Exceeded that in all his land!
With rasping breath and bulging eyes
And pounding heart, he knew that he
Would sell his soul to own these jewels
And pay the price with treachery.

He asked them, then, what they proposed.
What did they want? Quite what, he asked,
Would earn him all these gems he'd seen?
There must be some specific task?
There was, they said. A simple thing –
An evening's work was all he'd trade
And if he did it stealthily
No one would guess the deal he'd made.

They said they knew that fish were caught
In summer when the days were fine
Then smoked and stored in one large hut
To last them through the wintertime.

Without those stores, then all would starve;
The sea which froze up to the shore
Would stop the village fishermen
From putting out to catch some more.

Within a month, the villagers
Would have no choice but to agree
To any deal which might bring food –
To yield to any enemy.
They'd readily lay down their arms
And surely would make no defence
If those who came brought not just spears,
But food for their deliverance.

It all seemed clear. His life was harsh.
He wanted more, and certainly
Had wondered how he might escape
This life of cold and poverty.
And now this lucky break appeared,
At once appealing to his greed.
He didn't need a second thought.
He seized the chance. At once agreed.

One winter's night when all was ice
He woke and slipped out from his bed
And, making sure he made no noise,
Went to the store, just as they'd said.
He stacked the hut with wood he'd saved
Especially for this very night
Then sparking flints across dry tinder
Set the stack of fuel alight.

He'd made his way back long before
The blazing store was ever found –
Ran with the rest and watched the flames
As burning timbers hit the ground.
He did his best to look distraught
To make them think his feelings true
And to this end (he felt quite proud)
He even shed a tear or two.

The villagers weren't stupid folk
And every one amongst them knew
The awful peril that they faced,
And just how little they could do.
They all felt sure that they would starve
But worked their hardest nonetheless
To find a way to save themselves,
Whilst meanwhile hoping for the best.

The traitor wasn't too concerned.
He knew that in a week or two
The enemy would all arrive
With not just arms, but foodstuff too.
As time went by, though, doubts appeared.
What could have made them come so late?
It couldn't, surely, be that they
Would leave him, starving, to his fate?

In three months, still they'd not arrived.
The traitor now could clearly see
They'd never planned to come at all,
Saw through their foul duplicity.
By eating scraps he'd tucked away
He barely managed to survive.
When spring arrived, he sat alone
For all the others there … had died.

The sea thawed out, and spring had come
Before some ships came into view.
The starving traitor went to meet
The longboats and their landing crew.
He begged for food in pleading tones
And fell before them on his knees.
The Mad Dog threw him gems and said,
"You've earned them – go ahead, eat these!"

Mad Dog raised his head and laughed
Then turned and left the broken man
To watch his tears of deep despair
Cascade like raindrops on the sand.
What good were diamonds? Rubies? Pearls?
These riches couldn't compensate
For what he'd done to all his friends
Repaying love with greed and hate.

He ate some fish caught from the streams,
Regained his fitness day by day
Until at last he had the strength
To load his boat and sail away.
Behind, he left the fishing fleet
Belonging to his friends, now gone.
Condemned to live a nomad life:
To wander through the seas alone.

He travelled south for many months
When suddenly a storm arose;
The highest seas and strongest winds
To which he'd ever been exposed.
Through driving rain he turned to shore
And crashed through waves to make his way
Around the foam on Renne's Rocks –
Sought shelter then in Cawsand Bay.

Next day, he went ashore to rest.
Some houses stood where now you'll find
The Plymouth pub you know so well
(It's called the Admiral MacBride).
The Plymouth people welcomed him,
And fed him bread they'd freshly baked
With local fish and local game
Washed down with frothy ale they made.

He settled to a quiet life –
He fished alone beneath the mast
Still plagued by guilt for all the sins
Committed in his recent past.
At night he scarcely slept a wink;
In troubled dreams he'd see his friends
Who'd speak to him accusingly,
Demanding that he make amends.

One day he found he couldn't bear
The awful burden any more.
He moored his boat off Wembury beach
And hurled his gems across the shore.
Then with a rock about his neck
He waded out into the sea.
"These gems, this rock, this sandy beach
Are surely worth far more than me."

He walked out till the icy waves
Which rolled their way from Plymouth Sound
Were splashing up around his face.
He'd take one breath, and soon be drowned.
Then all around the water boiled,
And eerie fog quite suddenly
Appeared – or so it seemed to him –
To well up from the very sea.

And through this fog appeared twelve ships;
Each travelled in the wake before
And made their way towards the man,
And dropped their anchors near the shore.
And on each boat a fisherman
Stepped up and stood along the side
And stared at him from ghostly decks
Which rolled and creaked upon the tide.

He looked in terror through the fog
And instantly he knew the boats.
Nor did it take a second glance
To recognize the fishing folk.
These were the friends whom he had left;
The ones who'd suffered at his hand
Who lay, a thousand miles away,
In icy graves of frozen land.

He all at once confessed his guilt
And told them how a bag of stones
Was traded for that land of theirs –
And even for their very bones.
He said his life was worthless now,
And that he'd thrown away his wealth.
And now, unless they killed him first,
He told them that he'd kill himself.

A ghostly figure made reply.
His punishment would be far worse
Than any death he could devise.
Eternal life would be his curse.
He'd know an awful loneliness,
He'd sit with ages rolling by.
How futile making friends would be
Who in a blink grew old and died.

He'd lift this curse in just one way:
By proving his remorse was true.
He'd sinned three ways and so, they said,
There were three things he'd have to do:
To pay back death, he'd save a life.
Then rescue one who'd been betrayed.
Not sell – but help the local folk
By giving some great wealth away.

With this, they went just as they came.
The fog, evaporating, left
A clear blue sky, a flat calm sea,
And not a ripple to suggest
Those ghostly things of which you've heard;
That here a dozen ships passed by
Nor that, in summer, fog had come
To hide the sun in darkened sky.

But like a giant church bell tolling
Echoed in his head three tasks.
And he could have eternal peace
Were he to do each, as they'd asked.
Some parts were easy – he'd long planned
To help those locals in distress.
But other parts were difficult.
How would he deal with all the rest?

Where could he find a life to save?
And where a man who'd been betrayed?
And where to come upon huge wealth
Which he could win, then give away?
How could he meet all these demands?
How was he ever to ensure
That he could help the local folk
And tend their sick for ever more?

And with this question, Bruno paused
Then told them that his tale was done.
Lord Hunter wasn't satisfied.
"But was his challenge ever won?
You cannot leave a yarn like that,
A story full of death and greed,
Without a happy ending. Tell us:
Did the fisherman succeed?"

Old Bruno fixed him with his gaze,
Rebuked him gently as he said:
"My story's true and will not end
Until that northern man is dead.
You might not recognize this man
To whom my lengthy tale attests.
So aid each sailor you should meet.
You might just help one find his rest."

REACHING SPAIN

THE next few days were pleasant ones.
The sea was calm, the air was warm –
In fact, they rapidly forgot
The violence of the early storm.
For meals, they'd cook the scores of fish
That Hunter caught fresh every day,
While Daisy watched them from the bow,
Her wind-blown fur stiff with salt spray.

The crew enjoyed this brief respite,
But all too soon a shout was heard.
Their destination wasn't far
For Doctor Edge had seen land-birds.
And sure enough, within the hour
The cliffs of southern Spain were seen.
Lord Hunter strangely knew each part –
He'd seen this coastline in his dream.

They slipped into the port that night.
The sails were furled, then neatly stowed;
Mad Morgan, on the battlements,
Not noticing the ship below.
Before they slept, the crew all talked
Of what the next few days would hold.
But never could they have foreseen
The days of poison, wine … and gold.

6 And Rescue One Who's Been Betrayed

ASHORE IN SPAIN

THE Spanish sun rose warm next morning,
Soaked the sky in dawn's soft light
Which bathed *The Arctic Tern* in gold,
Her burnished timbers glowing bright.
Birds chirruped in the palms around
As traders came to set their stalls;
Fresh fish, or herbs, or vegetables
All sold beneath the castle walls.

Now the warming rays of morning
Soaked the boat and seeped within:
Roused them gently from their slumbers,
Aided by the shoreline din.
Though they'd settled down exhausted,
Tired from toil beneath the mast,
Now they woke with some excitement
For, today, they'd start their task.

From the deck there drifted down
The heavy smell of fresh-baked yeast.
Shopping from the stalls already,
Bruno had laid out a feast!
Dripping butter, jugs of juices,
Jams and fruits he'd all prepared.
Wave-made splintered sunrays showered them
As they ate their breakfast there.

Bruno had been hard at work,
And how his night-time toil now showed!
He'd hoisted Daisy overboard
And scrubbed her fur until it glowed.
He'd combed it straight, and now it looked
So clean that Hunter even joked
That given just a minute more
They'd see reflections in her coat!

The dog was not the only one
To whom he'd tended by the dawn.
This, they scarcely could believe:
The captain's head itself was shorn!
He'd combed out knots, and trimmed his beard
And plastered down each errant hair.
Of all the captains in Seville,
He surely was the smartest there!

He'd also donned a naval coat
With gleaming buttons and gold braid.
An anchor badge upon the front,
A brand new cap was on his head.
The Spanish king and noblemen
Would surely have to be impressed
By any seaman of such rank –
Especially one so finely dressed!

The others took the lead he'd set,
All anxious not to fail their queen.
They'd be the noblest group of men
The Spanish court had ever seen!
Before they left, they gathered up
The scroll and brooch they'd thought to bring
As proof of their goodwill, and which
They hoped they might give to the king.

So, thus attired, they made their way
Up through the narrow streets that led
Beside the waterside and on
Towards the castle up ahead.
But as they left the docks behind
They couldn't help but be aware
That something didn't feel quite right.
A heavy sadness filled the air.

Upon the battlements, they saw
The flags all flying at half-mast.
The castle guards were dressed in black
And took no notice as they passed.
The group were anxious. Something wrong?
The flags. Black clothes. Had someone died?
A coup? A trap? They reached in reflex –
Though no swords hung by their sides.

Arriving at the castle gates
They told the sentries why they'd come,
Explaining that they couldn't leave
Until their duties had been done.
The English queen herself, they said,
Had sent a message for the king.
They'd promised that no other man
Should see the scroll – no man but him.

The guards conferred, then let them in
And searched them – just in case they meant
To do some harm, and sabotage
Was actually their true intent.
The guards addressed them each in turn.
"What's the job you do?" they asked.
The captain, cook and lord replied,
With Doctor Edge explaining last.

At this, the guards all spoke at once,
Excited by the news that here,
Besides a seaman, cook and lord,
An Oxford doctor had appeared!
At once they told of how their king
Was dying; that their doctor knew
No more of what the diagnosis was
Than what, to cure him, he might do.

Would Doctor Edge be good enough
To see their king that very day?
For time was short, and all of them
Were sure he'd shortly pass away.
"Of course," said Edge, "I'll help your king.
To aid the sick where'er they're found,
To tend the ill and ease their pain,
By oath and honour I am bound."

With that, they hurried to a door
Which opened on some steps of stone
And climbed towards the battlements
To reach the room where lay the throne.
'Twas in this room the king was nursed
Upon a bed he'd had brought there.
The windows overlooked the port.
The room was filled with warm sea air.

Entering they saw at once
The king, who lay collapsed in bed.
So shallow were his gasping breaths
They thought at first that he was dead.
Edge hastened to the dying man
Whose body was so very thin
That bones stuck out at every point
Through wasted flesh and frosted skin.

DOCTOR EDGE
AND THE KING

QUICKLY, Edge called all his friends,
And beckoned to the guards around.
"No time to lose! The king will die
Unless a treatment can be found!"
With that, he seized a quill and parchment
Scrawled a list of herbs in haste.
"I must have these to make a cure.
Go now!" he said. "No time to waste!"

Calling to the household staff
He told them they must fetch a reed,
A gourd and some fresh water too
Along with salts that he would need.
They did exactly as he said,
Accepted orders readily
For they could see he knew his job
And knowledge gives authority.

Within an hour, they'd all returned.
He measured out the herbs he'd sought
And ground them in the mortar bowl
With salts and water which they brought.
The household, one by one, arrived
To watch the doctor as he'd try
To save the king they loved so much,
Who otherwise would surely die.

He poured the liquid from the mortar,
Strained through muslin to the gourd
And from a bundle, chose a reed
Then asked the guard to bring a sword.
Against it, now, the reed was sharpened
Then – and some thought this insane –
He seized the forearm of the king
And slipped the reed into a vein.

A common practice in that day
Meant cutting patients so they'd bleed.
Not Doctor Edge, who planned to give
His herbal medicine through a reed.
He thus knelt down beside the bed
And through the reed dripped medicine
Until at last the final drops
Had reached the royal blood within.

An hour went by. The household watched.
Then some of them began to cry,
For this must be a miracle:
The king improved before their eyes!
Still clearly sick, his skin was moist,
His eyes no longer deep and glazed.
Within an hour, this doctor's work
Had made him better than for days!

A REUNION FOR HUNTER

JUST at that moment, heads all turned
As someone swept in through the door;
A nobleman, they might have guessed,
To judge by all the silks he wore.
Just in time, he saw the crowd
And slipped a crown from off his head
(Indecent haste would not seem good:
He'd wait until the king was dead).

It seemed they knew him, liked him too,
For servants all around them bowed.
But Daisy, at Lord Hunter's feet,
Just bared her teeth, and snarled and growled.
A guard, saluting him, announced,
"Lord Morgan, merchant, and our heir."
Lord Hunter, though, knew him at once …
He knew the pirate standing there!

For Hunter well remembered him,
That face burned in his memory –
The Mad Dog who had sunk his ship
And tried to bury him at sea.
Good fortune, though, was his that day
For though they stood there eye to eye,
The Mad Dog didn't recognize
The captain whom he thought had died.

Lord Hunter found himself bemused.
What could have brought the Mad Dog here?
How had a common thug become
A powerful Spanish courtier?
And worse, if then the king had died
(As well he might with Edge not there)
It seemed from what the guard had said
That Morgan was the Spanish heir!

Whatever else it might have been,
It wasn't chance he held such sway.
What had Morgan done to get here,
Standing where his sick king lay?
He'd have to speak with Doctor Edge
At any opportunity.
What had made the king so ill?
And were there signs of treachery?

Morgan was himself confused.
That morning, just a glance could tell
The king would surely die by noon.
Oh yes, the plan was going well!
He'd felt like shouting out for joy
But somehow he had masked his glee
And wrung his hands, had sobbed and wept
In quite convincing misery.

He'd thought he'd have a drink, maybe,
And wait until the morning passed,
And then, he'd hoped, return to find
His "noble king" had breathed his last.
His years of scheming would pay off.
The castle, colonies and power,
Great wealth, the throne, this crown he held,
Would all be his within the hour!

Returning, something seemed amiss.
The crowd, it's true, was round the bed
Just as he'd pictured it would be
If summoned when the king was dead.
But no one seemed to be distressed.
In fact, on coming through the door
He noticed smiles. And worse than this,
The king looked *better* than before!

He felt a tightness in his chest.
He couldn't catch his breath. He swayed.
This couldn't be! What had become
Of all the plans that he had made?
And then he noticed strangers there.
What did they want? Who could they be?
And why, with one, was he aware
Of strange familiarity?

The guards mistook his shock for joy
So gripped was he with frank alarm.
They ran to help the swaying lord
And led him gently by the arm.
They sat him down, and said they'd known
Their prayers were answered, and that fate
Was on their side, when they first saw
Four Englishmen approach the gate.

Now Morgan heard how Doctor Edge
Had worked a miracle indeed
With herbs and water, salts and such
Delivered through a hollow reed.
At this he had to force a smile
Despite the fact that, deep inside,
He felt no happiness at all
To find his ruler still alive.

He had to act. But what to do?
He'd rather die than e'er allow
The scheme on which he'd worked so long
To come so far then falter now.
He couldn't just dismiss these men,
Such action would invite dissent.
Far from it. He would welcome them
Then make their absence *permanent*.

He therefore stood and praised Chris Edge
And all the friends with whom he came.
He welcomed them with open arms
And thanked them on behalf of Spain.
He asked them if they'd honour him
By not returning to the sea;
Instead remain, accept from him
Some Spanish hospitality?

By nightfall, then, they'd settled in.
Grand staterooms had been found for all,
And even Daisy had a place
On cushions set out in the hall.
But Doctor Edge declined a room
And asked that rugs be brought instead
And laid out on the marble floor;
He'd sleep beside his patient's bed.

By morning, Edge was feeling tired
Through tending to his patient's health.
The king improved and slept quite well –
Edge hardly got a wink himself!
But nonetheless he felt relieved
To find that, by the morning light,
The king looked so much better now
Than when the sun went down last night.

At eight o'clock Lord Morgan came
And humbly said he'd do his share
In caring for his stricken king
And play his part in nursing care.
Edge left, but glanced back from the door
As Morgan started pouring sips
Of some sweet Spanish wine he'd brought
Between the sleeping monarch's lips.

A Plan Conceived

THE doctor went to find his friends.
He didn't want to make a fuss,
But medically he'd noticed things
Which urgently they should discuss.
He found them in the banquet hall.
A meal quite fit for heads of state
Was laid out there – great mounds of fruit
And sweetmeats piled upon each plate.

Edge joined them for a hearty meal,
But secretly he slipped a note
Across the table to his friends:
There's danger! Meet me on the boat!
They nodded, and said nothing then,
But after breakfast made their way
Beyond the castle walls and down
To where their wooden vessel lay.

Once there, Lord Hunter took the chair
And said he also had concerns
But first they'd hear the doctor speak
Who'd tell them all of what he'd learned.
Edge stood, and paced the cabin deck.
"I don't know who would do this thing
But clear as day, a traitor's hand
Is poisoning the Spanish king!

"The symptoms and the signs are clear;
No other thing has made him sick.
His food or drink is laced for sure
With deadly poisonous arsenic!
We have to flush the traitor out,
And each of us must try to find
A way to halt the king's supply,
For he'll recover, given time."

A quiet smile crossed Bruno's lips.
Perhaps this was a chance to save
A very special sort of life –
The life of one "who'd been betrayed".
Lord Hunter stood then with a grin,
Announced that they might be surprised
To learn that he already knew
The man who threatened royal lives!

Of course, the others all had heard
Of how Lord Hunter once escaped
A death at sea in pirate hands,
How Bruno saved him from that fate.
"I'd not forget that pirate's face,
Would know him if we met again.
Lord Morgan and that evil man
I tell you, are one and the same!

"Although I know the traitor's name,
He's bound to say in his defence
That claims like these are quite absurd.
If true, where is the evidence?
We have to somehow prove his guilt
But stop him doing any harm;
But nothing that we say or do
Should cause him even slight alarm."

They sat together for a while,
As each tried hard to make a plan
To stop Mad Morgan's evil scheme
But meanwhile not alert the man.
The cook piped up. Had he heard right?
And was he really right to think
That poison only reached the king
Mixed in his food or in his drink?

If that were true, it seemed to him
That drink must be the likely way;
The most the king could do was sip –
He can't have eaten now for days.
"I'll volunteer to be a cook
And in the kitchen check what's passed
Through every bottle, vat or bowl
To end up in his drinking glass.

"Meanwhile, I think that one of us
Should always stay and watch the king.
Between us, we can keep him safe
From any further poisoning.
And finally, I also think
That Daisy should remain there too.
I know no better guard than she;
She's loyal, tireless, brave and true."

The logic was impeccable.
They all agreed with Adrian
That these suggestions, put together,
Made a truly first-rate plan!
So one by one they left the boat
All keen at once to make a start,
While Daisy, trotting on behind,
Seemed happy that she'd play her part.

DISCOVERY

BACK at the castle, the plan was beginning.
They sat down with Morgan to eat at midday
Then Hunter arose, banged the table for silence
And said to them all that he'd something to say.
He felt much aggrieved that a lowly ship's cook
Should be treated the same as a lord such as he.
More fitting that Adrian serve in the kitchen;
Lord Morgan, he hoped, would be pleased to agree?

Now Morgan thought this was a splendid idea,
To embarrass a servant in front of them all
So he quickly agreed, and at once called the guards
To drag Adrian out from the banqueting hall.
"I'm sorry," he said, "for the fact that this man
Should embarrass you all by the way he's behaved.
You can now be assured that he'll just do his job;
No longer a 'lord', he's now back as a slave."

And so it was easy to start on the plan.
With Adrian now well installed as a cook
He was able to keep a close eye on the servants
And check all the drinks that the sickly king took.
Meanwhile, Doctor Edge had announced his intention
To sleep by the king, and ensure someone stayed
In the room at all times to administer medicines
And tend him, and bathe him, and act as nursemaid.

The pile of silk cushions were moved from the hallway
And laid on the throne, on which Daisy would sleep.
Being banned, back at home, from beds, chairs or carpets,
To sleep on a *throne* was a wonderful treat!
All the while Mad Dog seethed, for this irksome intrusion
Could easily leave him with all his plans wrecked.
But he couldn't complain lest his motives were questioned
And one of the household might come to suspect.

In the following days Doctor Edge kept a watch
And was cunning in all that he did for the king.
He would take all the food and the drink that was brought
But would secretly throw it away in the bin.
Captain Bruno, in turn, would come visiting often
With fresh fruit and vegetables hidden each time
Which he'd pass to the doctor when no one was looking
Along with a bottle of replacement wine.

With careful attention and all Edge's medicines,
The signs of improvement were steady and sure.
Although much relieved, this made Edge very anxious
For he didn't want Morgan to know of the cure.
As soon as the king was of sound enough mind,
Doctor Edge spoke in detail of all that had passed.
He said that the king should pretend to be dying
Should anyone enter, or questions be asked.

The king was astonished and shocked by the news.
He couldn't believe that Lord Morgan was blamed –
That this man who had nursed him throughout recent weeks
And a murdering cur could be one and the same.
Nonetheless, he agreed that he'd follow advice
And would do everything that the doctor had asked –
For if innocent, then Morgan's name would be cleared
But if guilty, the king could then take him to task.

Meanwhile, in the kitchen, young Adrian worked
For the plan gave each one of them tasks they must do.
So he slaved at his cooking, but watched from the shadows,
Made efforts to find how the poison got through.
He noted quite quickly that fresh food was purchased
From different people or markets each day
And that no one complained if he cooked it himself
Or delivered it up to the king on a tray.

The food, he decided, was probably safe.
Of the drink, he was logically forced to suspect
That the wine must be poisoned; but strangely he saw
That the servants could drink it without ill effect.
He nearly gave up in despair more than once
For he just couldn't see how the traitor arranged
For the poison to get to the king. Then one night
He observed something happen which seemed very strange…

In the hope that he might catch the culprit red-handed,
He'd taken to hiding himself out of sight
By the side of a stove (which could be very hot!)
Where he'd rest, huddled up, through uncomfortable nights.
At about two o'clock, while the household all slept,
He awoke to the sound of a creak from the door
And the sound of soft footsteps, as someone came quietly
And furtively tiptoed across the stone floor.

Now Adrian froze, and at once held his breath
As the stranger stood silent and listened for sound,
The visitor snooped round the kitchen and pantry
In case there was anyone else still around.
At last he seemed satisfied no one was watching.
He walked to a door and undid the locks
Slipping out down some steps to return minutes later,
Then walked to the table and laid down a box.

Not five minutes later, more footsteps were heard
And the first man turned round as a second walked in.
Though the face of Lord Morgan was hidden in shadows,
Still Adrian knew straight away it was him.
The first man was also well known in the castle –
And Adrian, even at night, knew him too:
He worked in the kitchen as "cook to the king" –
'Twas the one Morgan called from his pirate ship's crew.

From the box he withdrew two full bottles of wine
Which were marked on the labels with small yellow dots.
In return, Morgan passed him a pair which were empty,
And these the cook took and then hid in the box.
The cook told Lord Morgan he'd added the poison
And each of the bottles now held three grains more.
Just a glass would now kill, and to mask the strong taste
He had made the wine sweeter than ever before.

Lord Morgan spoke briefly. He'd planned that the king
Should have regular doses of poison in wine.
In this way, his illness would come on quite slowly,
And no one would think Morgan caused his decline.
But now, with these Englishmen nursing the king,
It proved hard to deliver a steady supply
Of the poisonous wine to the lips of the king –
So he'd mixed a strong dose to be sure that he died.

Adrian listened. From what he could hear
It seemed Morgan had hoped for a steady decline.
But with Edge's attentions, he'd not found a way
To deliver small doses in regular wine.
But now, with its heavier lacing of poison,
He'd take both the doctor and monarch a drink
Whereupon both would die in a matter of hours
Of something contagious, so people would think.

Their evil plan laid, both the cook and Lord Morgan
Laughed quietly together, then made for the door
Whilst Adrian listened, heard creaking of hinges
Then tiptoeing footsteps across the stone floor.
He waited a while to be sure they had gone
Then, with joints stiff from sitting, he left the same way.
With heart pounding loudly, he fretted all night.
He'd somehow to warn all his friends the next day.

At breakfast next morning, whilst serving their table
He tripped "accidentally" where Hunter was sat –
Poured a jug of fresh orange juice over his friend
And then slipped him a note as he mopped at his lap.
Lord Hunter cursed loudly and left for his chambers,
Unfolded the letter and read it with haste.
Returned, unsuspected, now knowing the danger
In which both the doctor and king had been placed.

The friends strolled in sunshine when breakfast was over
And, whispering, Hunter told all that he knew.
Doctor Edge told the king how they'd come by the knowledge
And what they now knew that Lord Morgan would do.
The king now believed that Lord Morgan was guilty,
For how else could Hunter have known of the times
When this merchant had tended him throughout his illness
And plied him with glasses of sweet-tasting wine?

There still was no proof that Lord Morgan was guilty;
The king said, without it, he wouldn't react.
He'd wait in his bed until poison was brought
And thus would the traitor be caught in the act.
The doctor tried hard to dissuade him. If cornered,
Lord Morgan would never give up, so he thought.
Edge knew men like these. They would rather die fighting
And take others with them, than ever be caught.

But the king had decided. They'd just have to wait.
He would do what was right; leave the outcome to fate.

THE TRAITOR CAUGHT

THE next days were tense as they waited for Morgan
To make his last efforts to usurp the crown.
The stakes were now high. They all knew the risks.
They couldn't stop now, though. The gauntlet was down.
Lord Hunter was put in a difficult spot,
For he wished at all times to keep guard on the throne.
But if Morgan should see him or Bruno around
He might notice the trap, and therefore back down.

The hours turned to days, and Lord Morgan did nothing,
Behaved to them all as a perfect host would.
He met them at meal times, and asked of their health,
And made sure every comfort was theirs, if he could.
They all thought that, maybe, he'd somehow got warning,
His strike now subjected to untold delay.
That night, though, as all were retiring to bed
Lord Morgan walked in with some wine on a tray.

In the room, Doctor Edge was alone with the king
When Lord Morgan arrived and then bowed to the bed.
The king could see clearly the small yellow dot
Which was marked on the label, as Adrian said.
Lord Morgan announced that he'd come with a nightcap:
No better a tonic, he said, at such times
Than an evening of friendship and good sleep to follow,
All aided by glasses of sweet Spanish wine.

The king smiled and nodded. He sat up, and said
That he felt so much better now Morgan was here.
A true friend indeed, he had only to come
And the throne room was filled all at once with good cheer.
He'd therefore be pleased if Lord Morgan would join them:
How rude it would be if the king slaked his thirst!
Instead he would pour a fresh glass from the bottle
And Morgan would honour him by drinking it first.

He handed a glass to Lord Morgan and nodded.
"My friend," said the king, "let us drink to your health!"
Lord Morgan's hand shook. All his plans lay in ruins.
He'd failed in his bid for the crown and its wealth.
The king's smile was frozen, and so was the doctor's;
They clearly had heard of his treacherous game.
He shattered the glass on the bedstead beside him.
The king and the doctor would die just the same!

He pulled out a dagger from under his cloak
And then rushed at the king with it over his head.
He no longer cared if they knew it was murder
His only concern was the king should be dead!
For a moment, it seemed that he might have succeeded
For the king, moving slowly, was sure to be harmed
When Daisy howled loudly and dived from the throne
To sink all her teeth, from mid-air, in his arm.

He screamed as the dagger was dropped from his grasp.
Daisy hung there and snarled (while still wagging her tail:
After all, she'd been given silk cushions and thrones,
And, completing her pleasure, a good fight as well!).
The more Morgan struggled and hit the poor dog,
The more determined she was she'd put up a show.
She'd stay there till Christmas if given the chance
And if Edge didn't stop her, might never let go!

The doctor ran quickly to tug at the bell-pull,
He hauled at it, summoning guards to arrive
Then he rushed at Lord Morgan and hurled himself forwards –
Crashed into his legs with an elegant dive.
They fell to the floor and were struggling there
With the dagger still lying not far out of reach;
Though it made little difference to Morgan, whose arm
Was held fast by Daisy, clamped on like a leech.

Bruno and Adrian followed the soldiers
With Hunter (they'd noticed the guards rushing past).
The king gave the orders, and Morgan was shackled
And led from the room with his arms firmly grasped.
The king, though quite shaken, stood up by his bed
And then thanked all his friends who had saved him that night.
Picking up Morgan's dagger, he asked them to kneel
And then dubbing their shoulders, made each of them knights.

That night, in the castle, a party was held.
Amidst all the noise Bruno slipped off alone –
On the deck, sat with Daisy, his constant companion,
Shared silence and stars and the soft coastal foam.
As the warm waters lapped, so his thoughts drifted with them.
He'd saved Hunter's life, and today "one betrayed".
But to help local folk and distribute great wealth…
Could this ever be done? Could his debts be repaid?

7 The Trial

RELAXATION

The months that came were paradise.

THE warm waves lapped the sun-soaked shore
And scented winds seeped through each door.
The nights were filled with food and rest
And all agreed, these were the best
Of days that they would ever share
And happily they rested there.
The king grew ever stronger now
And walked each day (if Edge allowed)
Along the seafront, past the stalls
Where joyful greetings came from all.

The crew were fêted by the crowds
Who sought to drape their necks in flowers
And pressed upon them gifts each day,
And with each present they would say
How much they owed these Englishmen
Who'd done such good for all of them.

And even Daisy found herself
Recipient of untold wealth –
More bones than any dog had seen
Outside the best of canine dreams!

The Arctic Tern, beside the shore,
Was somehow different from before;
The fittings, once of tarnished brass
Now glinted as of gold and glass.
Her paintwork shone as if brand new,
Her mast looked newly polished too.
Quite how such changes came to be
Remained a total mystery;
The crew were baffled to a man,
Though Bruno seemed to understand.
He'd sometimes smile as he'd inspect
The glowing timbers of the deck.

Beneath the castle on the hill
Which overlooked this town, Seville
Lay many dungeons – cold dank rooms
Off miles and miles of catacombs,
And townsfolk could be heard to tell
How these were used as prison cells.
In truth, the king would not condone
Or order from his regal throne
The use of these facilities
For any purpose such as this.
No matter what his crime might be,
Each man should keep his dignity.

In comfort, then, above the gate
Lord Morgan sat, consumed with hate.
From windows, he'd hear people sing
The praises of both crew and king
And bitterly he'd curse these curs,
These interfering foreigners!

His evil mind at once was set.
He hadn't been defeated yet!
He'd bide his time, would find a way
To take revenge another day
And in some future time and place
He'd wipe the smile off every face.

He thus pretended to the guards
That now he'd had a change of heart;
Regretted what he'd done, and would
Redress the balance if he could.
He begged them to stand up in court
And tell the king that they now thought
His punishment should never be
A life in jail. Could they not see?
A better sentence at the trial
Would be a life spent in exile;
He'd then be free to help the poor,
Repent for what had gone before.

A month went by before the king
Was well enough to set a date
On which a jury would be called
To judge the man, decide his fate.
Until that time, Lord Morgan tried
Much harder with each passing day
To make the guards believe he'd changed,
And tried to make them use their sway.

The crew, meanwhile, enjoyed their stay.
As weeks went by they all agreed
That soon the king would be quite well
And then would be the time to leave.
It fell to Edge to set a time.
Although he couldn't say for sure
He thought that by Lord Morgan's trial
The king would need his help no more.

The king consulted with them all,
Accepting what they had to say
And thanked them for the help he'd had
And that they had agreed to stay.
He asked that they attend the trial
As many there might hold a grudge.
Impartial to the state's affairs,
They'd see Lord Morgan fairly judged.

Excitement mounted in the port.
The citizens were keen to see
How king and jury would behave
And what the sentence was to be.
For since the king had come to power
No criminal had met his fate
By torture, floggings or the rack
Nor execution by the state.

But surely this must be the case
Where noble thoughts would soon give way
To vengeance by the king himself,
Who'd make sure Morgan's debt was paid?
The people guessed the king would call
For Morgan to be hanged; he'd see
That any man who crossed him thus
Would pay the price for treachery.

With drums that beat like pounding hearts
And fanfares, so the trial date came.
And in the courtroom, packed with colour,
Crammed, it seemed, the whole of Spain.
A silence settled. All arose.
The king walked, solemn, down the aisle
With courtiers, then the Englishmen,
Following in single file.

A moment later came the guards
Escorting Morgan wrapped in chains.
For sympathy, he dragged one foot
And shook his head as if in pain.
His gaze directed to the floor,
He feigned a look of misery.
He turned towards the throne and bowed;
How well he faked humility!

The court was read the evidence.
And all were shocked at what they heard.
As in a theatre, not in court,
They hissed and booed at every word!
They learned of Morgan's other life;
Of how he'd lived from piracy,
Of how he'd once sunk Hunter's boat
And left him there to drown at sea.

They heard how Morgan killed the chef
And brought his pirate cook instead;
Plied the king with poisoned wine,
Would take the throne when he was dead.
The crowd drew breath, some even cheered
– In fact, they burst into applause –
When told how Daisy saved the day
With nothing else but teeth and claws.

When all was said, the king arose.
Lord Morgan's guilt was clear as day,
But was there anything at all
The prisoner might wish to say?
For every man should have his chance
To stand and plead his innocence;
To face the men accusing him
And speak some words in self-defence.

Lord Morgan rose and cleared his throat
(Pretending to be choked with guilt)
And shook with fear and frank remorse
(Emotions which he'd never felt).
He said he had no good excuse,
His guilt was plain for all to see.
But he'd seen the error of his ways
And pleaded now for clemency.

The king now stood and turned. He paused
Before he'd say another word;
He'd thank his friends for all they'd done,
The heroes of the tale they'd heard.
If Englishmen behaved like this
He'd gladly have them all as friends.
From this time forth, they had his pledge:
The feud with Spain was at an end.

And in that spirit, he would show
That peace was better than a war.
A man, if wronged, must set aside
His anger at what's gone before.
Lord Morgan would walk free that day –
Indeed, he'd take a bag of gold
And live in exile from the land
To help the poor, the sick, the old.

With that, the king called to the guards
To loose the chains that held the man
And take him to his boat near by,
And see it safely far from land.
And just before he left the room,
He shook Lord Morgan's hand and said
That he forgave him all he'd done;
To others he must pay his debt.

Lord Morgan packed, and in disgrace
Was walked by guards down to the sea.
The townsfolk watched him board his ship
And glared in silence from the quay.
He hoisted sails, sailed from the port,
And as he left the Spanish shore
He raised the pirate flag aloft:
He'd take revenge, on that he swore!

8 Not Take – But Give Great Wealth Away

GOING HOME

A WEEK after this, and the Englishmen packed.
The time had now come when they had to return.
Their mission was finished. The queen would be waiting;
Of peace with the Spanish she shortly would learn.
Before they had gone, though, the king called them in
And privately thanked them for all they had done;
The debt which he owed them could not be repaid
And he cared for them all as if each were a son.

He handed Lord Hunter a scroll of pale parchment
He'd sealed with red wax and a ribbon of gold.
It offered full peace with the English in future,
And in it the tale of their valour was told.
He'd made it quite clear that he might not have trusted
Ambassadors, messengers … men of that kind.
But these were unlike any men he had known.
It was through their compassion this treaty was signed.

And now to Old Bruno he turned and spoke softly.
Twelve ships, in a dream, he'd seen moored in the bay.
The captain of one had walked up to the bow
And had beckoned him over. He had this to say:
"You must take out a chest – get the biggest you have –
And then fill it with silver and pieces of eight.
You must give it to Bruno to carry away,
He will know what to do; it's his means of escape."

Now Edge thanked the king for his words and the scroll,
Said the pleasure of helping was truly their own.
They'd little to leave as a gift from them all
To a man with the wealth which belonged to the throne!
Even so, they would leave him a token of friendship –
His wife, he explained, made a brooch with great pride;
'Twas her finest creation, in silver and gold,
With the heads of his daughters arranged side by side.

The doctor bowed deeply. The king took the gift
And wore it with pride from that day to his last.
Such brooches were soon thought the height of good taste;
You can see them in paintings of centuries past.
They were made in both silver and gold, and enamel,
And porcelain versions were soon to abound;
They had heads set in white, on a background of blue.
In museums and jewellers' today they're still found.

But Bruno was silent. He'd met great success
But this treasure presented unlocked freedom's door.
He'd take it to England, then give it away
For the good of the locals, the sick and the poor.
He hoped, in this way, that three wrongs would be righted.
In rescuing Hunter, a life had been saved.
He could now give great wealth and so help the needy –
The last of the tasks now he'd saved one betrayed.

TREACHERY AGAIN

B Y night-time the chest had been loaded aboard,
And the struggle meant all of the townsfolk now knew
What the chest must contain. And the word of these riches
Reached not just the honest, but evil men too.
And from a dark corner, a trader was watching;
He'd only that day come and set up his stall.
And, strangely for someone who seemed to be selling,
He didn't display any items at all.

He carried a constant companion beside him,
A parrot that lived in a large iron cage.
With green and gold feathers, but cold evil eyes,
If disturbed, it would hiss or would squawk in a rage.
Just as well for this man that, barring Lord Hunter,
Mad Morgan ensured all the sailors had died
When he'd plundered those vessels; for any such crewmen
Would recall the trader at Mad Morgan's side.

On the arm of the trader was found a tattoo,
'Twas an octopus glaring with fiery red eyes.
An image that Hunter at once would have known
For it flew on the pirate flag raised to the skies.
For this innocent trader was really a pirate,
A spy who'd been sent to be sure Morgan learned
Of such time as the Englishmen seemed to be packing
To leave on their vessel – the ship *Arctic Tern*.

On hearing that treasure was now being loaded,
The pirate decided his master must know.
He opened the cage of his beady-eyed parrot
And whispered to her that she'd soon have to go.
He wrote out a letter in which he explained
That the Englishmen's boat carried treasure aboard;
By nightfall, the crew would have made preparations,
And surely, at dawn, they'd set sail for abroad.

He fastened the note round the leg of the parrot;
Released her to fly back to Lord Morgan's hands
So he'd learn that same day of the news from Seville
And could quickly react and prepare detailed plans.
Now Morgan, till then, had but one aim in life:
He had wanted to ambush and sink Bruno's boat.
But he spotted the chance to do better than that
When that evening the parrot arrived with the note.

His vessel was hidden within a small cove
Not a half-hour away from where Bruno's was moored.
He sailed, then, at midnight – by one had arrived.
He dropped anchor; a longboat was slipped overboard.
Six pirates crouched low by the sides of the boat
And they silently paddled their way 'cross the sea
Past a sleeping Seville and along through the harbour
Then clambered their way up the walls of the quay.

In shadow, the men crept towards Bruno's boat
Where stood guards, whom the king had insisted be left.
They were tired from the work which they'd done through the day
And the effort of loading the full treasure chest.
It was therefore quite easy to sneak down the quay
And from there they were able to launch their attack.
They boarded the ship in a matter of seconds.
The guards they'd knocked out were left trussed up in sacks.

A longboat was moored to *The Arctic Tern*'s bow
And was loaded with treasure heaved over the side.
They strapped it down safely, pushed off from the *Tern*,
Then, rowing in silence, slipped out on the tide.
The Arctic Tern lay on a glassy sea surface;
There wasn't a wave, and no breath of wind stirred.
Yet gently at first, then with increasing fury,
She rolled and she pitched, and her bell was soon heard.

Above, in the castle, Old Bruno was sleeping
What woke him that night he could not really say.
His breath short and quiet, he sat and he listened;
The sound of a bell drifted up from the bay!
The rest of his crew had themselves been awoken
And rushed from their rooms, and descended the stairs.
Grabbing bags as they went, they ran out of the castle
And burst through the gate to the cold morning air.

Seized with fear, Bruno panicked – he knew right away
That the chest had been stolen while he was asleep.
He had given his word that he'd give wealth away,
And this promise was one he intended to keep.
His freedom demanded he cared for the sick,
That he went to the rescue of one man betrayed.
He'd succeeded in that, saved the life of the king;
Till he'd sacrificed wealth, though, his debt wasn't paid.

Sure enough, at the boat, all the guards were trussed up.
When released, they explained that six men had appeared.
They had recognized one as a close friend of Morgan's;
The chest had been stolen, as Bruno had feared.
He asked when it happened – they must be precise –
Just how long had it been since all this had gone on?
They were told that the pirates had only just left;
It was not half an hour since their boat must have gone.

Only twelve hours before had the treasure been loaded,
Yet Morgan had heard, and had stolen the chest.
They'd sneaked in by longboat. These facts all suggested
He must be close by to have managed the theft.
They'd ready their boat, and must put out to sea!
They'd give chase to the pirates wherever they'd run!
They'd take what was theirs, and defeating Mad Morgan.
They'd do what was right, and see justice was done!

THE CHASE

AS one, they leapt aboard the ship –
They couldn't waste a moment's time.
With Adrian behind the wheel,
Lord Hunter slashed the mooring lines.
Bruno hauled to hoist the sails,
Sweat on his forehead as he scowled
While Daisy, standing on the bow,
Drew breath, then raised her head … and howled.

By now, the pirate thieves were back,
Had hauled their booty to the deck,
When suddenly Lord Morgan froze:
The hairs were prickling on his neck.
A ghostly howl had reached his ears
(Though, strangely, not those of his men)
And never had he felt such fear
As that which welled within him then.

The Arctic Tern was after him –
He knew the truth instinctively.
And this time, if they captured him,
He'd not slip free so easily.
He panicked – knew he had to run
And find some lonely hiding place.
Sail south, perhaps to Africa
And soon lose Bruno in the chase.

With parrot perched upon his arm
And skull and crossbones flying high,
He raised the anchor, set the sails,
Turned east as dawn lit up the sky.
Pathetic people! Fools to think
They'd catch him quite that easily.
He'd teach them not to mess around
With such a shrewd adversary!

The Arctic Tern by now was off;
A wind had risen suddenly
Which wrenched the sails and sped the boat
Through spume and surf and mounting seas.
But which way should they go from here?
Lord Hunter shouted in despair.
They'd never get the treasure back,
For Morgan could be anywhere.

His spirit broken, Hunter wept.
He sank down, beaten, to his knees
When through the darkness, clear as day,
He heard the voice of dear Louise.

"Think of me should you feel helpless
Lost, or when you feel alone.
Call my name; the love we share
Will guide you safely back to home."

Eyes shut, he called to dear Louise
And through her sleep she heard his words.
And in her dreams she answered him;
She stood. Released a black-capped bird.
Lord Hunter stood, walked to the bow,
Then turned his head towards the skies
And there appeared the self-same bird
Which rode the wind before his eyes.

He called to Bruno. "Trust me now;
I cannot tell you how I know,
But following that bird you see
Will take us where we need to go!"
Old Bruno swung the helm around
And chased the rays of dawn's first light.
The Arctic Tern was rushing east
As Daisy howled into the night.

Lord Morgan's temper now was frayed.
Despite the waves brought by the squall,
The wind behind them for an hour,
They moved at snail's pace, if at all.
And through this time he'd heard those howls
From Bruno's dog – and now the din
Grew louder as each minute passed;
They'd followed, and were closing in!

How could they trail his every move?
How had they known which way to head?
They seemed to know where he had moored,
And also, which way he had fled!
But still he'd fool them – turn around,
And unlit by the morning sun
He'd sneak right past them in the dark
And head back west the way he'd come.

Aboard *The Arctic Tern*, the crew
Were sailing with the bird in sight,
When suddenly it banked above
And turned south-west. That wasn't right!
But Hunter told them not to fear –
The pirate boat had doubled back
In efforts to evade the chase
And throw the hunters off the track.

Just as they turned, the wind swung too
And rushed with force from Spanish shores.
It filled the sails, and heeled them over,
Driven faster than before.
And now, just as the sun appeared
Old Bruno took his telescope
And, following the bird above,
He caught a glimpse of Morgan's boat.

From high up on the pirate mast
Lord Morgan's lookout yelled; he'd seen
The Arctic Tern not far behind,
And gaining with alarming speed!
Lord Morgan twitched. His face went white.
His body dripped with icy sweat.
Deep down, he knew the game was lost
But still, he'd not give in just yet!

So, all that day Lord Morgan fled.
His ship ran south before the gale
And made the greatest speed she could
By hoisting each and every sail.
His crew threw all they had away
To make the vessel travel light.
Perhaps they might maintain their lead
And lose Old Bruno in the night…

Lord Morgan's confidence now grew.
His glimpses of the stormy stars
Made clear that now the northern coast
Of Africa could not be far.
Here, under cover of the night,
They'd slip through waters he knew well.
Old Bruno, if he dared pursue,
Would run aground in coastal swell.

Bruno guessed the plan at once.
It seemed that they were coastal-bound
Where razor reefs and unseen shoals
Could see them driven fast aground.
He therefore went below the decks
And locked his cabin door behind
And, lying in his hammock there,
He tried to bring old friends to mind.

And in his thoughts, he spoke to them.
He'd tried his best – succeeded too;
He'd saved the life of one betrayed
Just as they'd told him he should do.
They'd also bade him tend the poor
And give great wealth away. At last
The chance to do these things had come;
But now was slipping from his grasp.

"I've learned my lesson. Hear me now,
For with your help I'll yet succeed.
Bring your boats, and turn him back
And help me in my hour of need!"
Deep down, he thought they wouldn't come.
He stood, then shook his head and sighed
Whilst at that moment, close at hand,
A fearsome sight met Morgan's eyes.

Mad Morgan stood completely stunned.
The sky now cleared, the stars ablaze
Yet up ahead, despite the wind
There seemed to come a growing haze.
In minutes, banks of fog built up
And from it – filling him with fear –
Twelve ghostly masts and sails arose
And under them, twelve boats appeared.

They left no wake and made no noise.
Their ghostly timbers glowing pale,
They seemed to float above the waves
And moved with ease against the gale.
And at the bow of every boat
A fishing captain gazed ahead
His arm outstretched accusingly.
There was no choice. Lord Morgan fled.

BRUNO'S LOSS

THE crew thought Morgan truly mad –
His words and actions quite absurd.
He said that he could "hear the dog" –
A noise not one of them had heard.
Quite why they fled, they couldn't see,
For normally he'd stand and fight,
But from this shabby English crew
He'd quaked with fear and taken flight!

He'd set one course, then change his mind;
The reasoning was hard to tell.
And now he'd swung towards the *Tern*
And sailed into the wind as well!
He screamed that they must "get away"
But what had caused him such alarm?
For miles around was empty sea
With nothing there to cause him harm…

The pirates, now, had had enough.
Lord Morgan had gone raving mad!
So while he struggled at the wheel
They gathered up what things they had
And crept away to make escape.
They dropped the longboat off the stern
Then leaped aboard and rowed away
From Mad Dog and *The Arctic Tern*.

So now, alone, Lord Morgan sailed,
And with each hour, frustration grew.
Curses on *The Arctic Tern*!
And curses on those twelve ships too!
For if he turned, Old Bruno's boat
Would spot this, and would alter course.
And if he went the other way,
Those ghostly ships would head him off.

There thus was little he could do;
He couldn't even set a course.
The way he went was not his choice
And every turn he made was forced.
But still, alone behind the wheel
He struggled on with little sleep.
He'd suffer anything at all –
Would rather die than face defeat.

Aboard *The Arctic Tern*, the men
Were jubilant with their success;
The north-west course on which they sailed
Was one which would retrace their steps!
If all went well, they'd soon be home,
And like a sheepdog with a flock
They'd guide Lord Morgan all the way
Until they'd moored in Plymouth docks.

And so it was, some four days on
As midday sun beat all around,
That Morgan and *The Arctic Tern*
Approached the edge of Plymouth Sound.
For all those miles the wind had howled
But as they came to Renne's Rocks
And neared the Shagstone, suddenly
The gale-force wind abruptly dropped.

Exhausted, hanging from the wheel,
Lord Morgan gazed in disbelief
As to one side the ghostly ships
Sailed on towards the rocky reef.
And as he stared, the vessels seemed
To slowly melt beneath the sun.
The masts dissolved – so too the mist;
The ships all gone … except for one.

For to the port *The Arctic Tern*
Rolled slowly as she lay becalmed.
So far away, without a breeze,
At least she couldn't cause him harm.
But as he watched, he shook his head;
For as each wave came rolling in
It carried Bruno's boat along
And drove it ever nearer him.

Old Bruno sighed. At last they'd won.
And as the ships and ghostly haze
Evaporated, so he felt
The tension of those recent days
Lift from his shoulders. Now he stood
And watched as gentle waves and tide
Licked their timbers, washed them gently
On towards Lord Morgan's side.

Adrian released the sails
And walked with Bruno to the bow.
Doctor Edge, and Hunter too,
Now surfaced from their bunks below.
The doctor took a grappling hook
And from his belt he hung his sword,
Prepared to hook Lord Morgan's boat
Then pull it in and go aboard.

Lord Morgan knew the game was up,
But even so, he'd make quite sure
That if he couldn't win this fight,
The treasure chest would stay aboard.
He hauled on ropes to raise a flag
And where the Jolly Roger flew
The octopus with fiery eyes
Upon a flag now hung there too.

He went below and took an axe
And sharpened up its blade of steel
Then swung it down repeatedly
And smashed a hole beside the keel.
As icy water flooded in
He climbed the stairs to reach the deck
And stood beside the treasure chest –
Trapped now aboard a sinking wreck.

And with the parrot on his arm
He stood beside the ship's bronze bell
And shouted to *The Arctic Tern*,
"You'll only catch me now in hell!
You thought that treasure would be yours:
Would soon be split between your crew.
Well, bad luck, I've got news for you!
If I can't have it, nor can you!"

They watched aghast as Morgan's boat
Now settled, and the upper decks
Were covered by the gentle waves,
Which shortly climbed to Morgan's neck.
He glared at Bruno to the last
And uttered not a further word.
In seconds now, the ship had gone:
The pirate flags the last submerged.

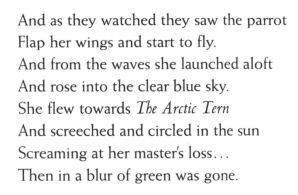

And as they watched they saw the parrot
Flap her wings and start to fly.
And from the waves she launched aloft
And rose into the clear blue sky.
She flew towards *The Arctic Tern*
And screeched and circled in the sun
Screaming at her master's loss…
Then in a blur of green was gone.

As Morgan's body was engulfed,
The water boiled about his face
And in the glare as Bruno watched
A transformation now took place.
Two fiery eyes glared out in red,
Eight tentacles seemed to appear;
An octopus writhed at the spot
There in the foam … then disappeared.

The Arctic Tern limped to the shore.
Her crew would have a tale to tell:
Of pirates, treachery and death;
Of castles, kings and gold as well.
But Bruno stood alone awhile.
He'd lost. And who knew if, or when,
That chance "to give great wealth away"
Would ever come to him again?

HOME AT LAST

THAT evening, ashore, a huge party was held
With a corner reserved at their pub the MacBride.
At the head of the table sat Bruno. As usual,
His coat had been placed on the floor by his side.
He ate his black rye-bread, fresh baked just that day,
And he supped from a tankard while facing the door
Not leaving a drop in his glass or his bottle,
A habit of which I have told you before.

Next day, in a carriage, they travelled to London –
Were met by royal guards and were led to the court
Where they bowed to the queen and, before her advisors,
Lord Hunter arose and then gave his report.
He spoke of Lord Morgan, and of his foul efforts
To murder the king and himself take the throne.
How Edge, as their doctor, had saved the king's life;
How the credit for this should be Edge's alone.

He told her how Adrian slept in the kitchens –
Discovered how Morgan concealed poisoned wine;
How, confronted, Lord Morgan had pulled out a dagger,
How Daisy had hung from his arm just in time.
He said that the merciful king had recovered.
The tale of the trial was then faithfully told;
How the king had insisted they take back to England
A treasure chest crammed with both silver and gold.

And finally, Hunter explained how the treasure
Was stolen by Morgan not five days before.
How *The Arctic Tern* chased him and – this bit was odd –
Had been able to steer him towards English shores.
They told how, at last, Morgan knew he was beaten
And scuppered the ship near the shore, off a reef
Known as Renne's Rocks then (just as now) to the locals:
How the Shagstone now marked where the ship came
   to grief.

The tale of adventure was ended. A silence
Descended on all who stood there in the court.
Lord Hunter stepped forward, then knelt by the queen
And delivered the scroll of pale parchment he'd brought.
And in it, the king said he might not have trusted
Ambassadors, messengers … men of that kind.
But these were unlike any men he had known.
It was through their compassion this treaty was signed.

The queen was delighted. Her faith was rewarded.
At last – peace with Spain! And to her it was clear
That the credit for this was not hers, but belonged
To the men (and the dog!) who were now standing here.
She drew Hunter's sword, bade them kneel, dubbed their shoulders;
"Arise now, brave knight!" she then said to each man.
(In fact, they were now knights of Spain and of England –
This record in honour is one which still stands.)

A week or so later, the coaches were loaded.
Before they all boarded, they swore from that day
That if Bruno should ever need help in the future
They would answer his call and would come right away.

Doctor Edge went to Oxford, where Jenny, his wife
Had been patiently waiting for him to return.
He was greeted with joy by his two little girls,
Both delighted to hear of the honours he'd earned.
The rest of his life he devoted to science
And never again did he go back to sea.
Jenny's business expanded with "By Royal Appointment"
The label she tied to her fine jewellery.

Lord Hunter went home to Louise in the north,
And without hesitation he begged for her hand.
They were married that month in a grand church in Durham;
The reception which followed was just as they planned.
And it has to be said that the party was good,
For both husband and wife were awake at the dawn.
They lived in the castle where, just nine months later,
Their first son, a boy they called Daniel, was born.

Adrian went back to Bridget his wife,
And in Rolvenden opened a place serving food:
He would cook it himself, and the customers came
For the freshly baked rye-bread, and ale that he brewed.
He lived out his days in this sleepy Kent village;
The restaurant stood only yards from the green.
If you go there, you'll find that the green still remains
And that Adrian's place, now a pub, is still seen.

Old Bruno went back to his fishing in Plymouth,
Where all of the locals were worried to see
How depressed he'd become since returning from Spain,
And how lonely and weary he now seemed to be.
He no longer went far – cast his nets out in Heybrook.
If asked, he would say he had only one wish:
He was fishing for timber of some sunken boat
And was hoping to catch silver coins and not fish.

The decades went by, and the young became old –
Just Old Bruno, his boat, and old Daisy remained.
The passage of time, though, did not seem to mark them;
One hundred years on, you'd have noticed no change.
And each evening you'd find him alone in the pub.
If you asked him for what he was waiting that day
He'd look up from his pint, and would say, "For the chance
To recover fortune, then give it away."

But Bruno could not let the treasure be lost.
He hadn't a choice, and someday he would try
To return to the wreck and discover the treasure.
He'd finish his task – and would find peace … and die.

BOOK THREE

Plymouth Not Long Ago

1 *Underwater*

FISHING FOR TREASURE

AS Bruno waited, mankind tried
To swim beneath the waves and find
The treasures which he thought must be
Beneath the surface of the sea.
In early days, he'd take a reed,
One hollowed out so he could breathe,
And in his mouth he'd hold it tight
And hope that in this way he might
Draw breath while swimming on the reef;
The tip above – his face beneath.

Still others tried to hold their breath
And, wearing flippers, plumb the depths
Until they'd have to make their way
From ocean gloom to light of day.
They ever deeper sought to go,
And sometimes carried weights below
To take them down with greater speed;
And in this way, aimed to succeed
In going deeper than before
With every venture from the shore.

Still others, weighted down with lead,
Put household buckets on their heads!
The buckets had been modified
Specifically that they might dive,
With rope to hold them, and glass too
To help them take a submerged view.
These home-made efforts, made of wood,
Thus formed a sort of makeshift hood
Whose air supply was pretty small.
With leaks, they weren't much use at all.

The same idea was later tried
With barrels lowered from the side
Of boats, from which old wrecks were sought
Wherein lay treasures – so they thought.
The weighted barrel would descend,
And from the barrel's open end
A diver could appear and swim;
When out of breath he'd go back in.
Pumped through a hose, fresh air would go
From boat to barrel down below.

Two men – the Deans – had some success
In salvaging great wealth from wrecks
And in the eighteenth century
They salvaged cannon from the seas.
They used a barrel and airhose
To dive a wreck – the *Mary Rose*.
With modern gear, the wreck was raised
And now, in Portsmouth, is displayed.
But with the cannon there on show
Are those the Deans brought from below.

It took two hundred years or more
Of trial, mistakes and deaths before
Two men, called Cousteau and Gagnan,
Designed an early aqualung.
They tried it first in open sea
In France in nineteen forty-three,
And using it they quickly found
That they could dive and swim around
And breathe through valves from tanks of air
Which, on their backs, they'd carried there.

With copied tanks and valves like these,
Still others found that they could breathe
And swim for hours quite happily
Beneath the surface of the sea.
They used it just for fun or sport
Until to some there came the thought
That with it they could salvage wrecks
And search for treasure, swim the decks
Of ships which lay beyond the reach
Of any land-bound man or beast.

In Plymouth was a man like this
Who'd made his living catching fish.
He'd lived there all his life – had been
A feature of the local scene
For longer than most could recall;
Known and loved by one and all.

In summer nineteen sixty-one
He'd bought an early aqualung;
A rubber wet suit, all in black,
With tanks to go upon his back.
Within a week or maybe two
He'd got the hang of what to do
And took to spending all free time
Indulging in his new pastime.

He trawled that winter, but next year
Abandoned nets and fishing gear.
Instead he kitted out his boat
With winches, hooks and miles of rope,
Thereafter spending every day
In diving kit round Heybrook Bay.

Each summer day, he'd walk along
The cobbles of the Barbican
And stop down by the waterside,
And in the Admiral MacBride
He'd sit and drink a pint of ale,
Eat fresh-baked bread. He'd then set sail
And hug the coast while running east
Past Bovisand and Wembury beach.

The local people saw that he
Would always, when he put to sea,
Head straightaway for Renne's Rocks
And once near by, prepare to drop
A length of rope to which was tied
An anchor with, hitched to its side,
A sack, from which was seen to float
Another ten yard length of rope.

With aqualung upon his back,
He'd dive below to where the sack
Hung inches from the ocean floor
Suspended from the anchor's claw
And then along a length of rope
(The ten-yard length of which we spoke)
He'd swim until he reached the tip
Which dragged, of course, behind the ship.

Abandoned to the wind and tide,
The fisherman now off the side,
The boat would drift along and tow
The man along, who far below
Had passed the sack beneath the ship
And to a rope had taken grip.

The fisherman would therefore scour
The seabed in each waking hour
And in this way could search with ease
A vast expanse beneath the seas
Where metal scrap, dumped in the war,
Lay littering the ocean floor.
For bombs and wire and metal plate
And engine parts all met this fate;
In wartime all this waste was tipped
Straight overboard from fighting ships.

Some parts of this were left to rust.
From others, he would earn his crust;
For iron, he cared not a jot,
But brass and lead were worth a lot.
Such metal, shining white or gold,
He'd spot and salvage to be sold.
He'd lift the piece, then swim right back
And dump it in the nearby sack.

And when the sack at last was full
He'd surface, clamber out, and pull
On winches till at last he'd see
The load appear, all draped in weed.
He'd lower it upon the deck
Would tip it out, and then inspect
The haul, and shortly he'd dump overboard
The worthless bits, and keep a hoard
Of metals he might sell, instead;
Like brass and bronze and tin and lead.

He'd take this scrap, and from its sale
Could buy his rye-bread and his ale
But never would he be as rich
As if he'd stuck to catching fish.
In fact, as all the locals saw,
These diving ventures left him poor;
He wore old clothes, could not afford
A place to live, so slept on board.

The locals had no sympathy
When each day he put out to sea;
They'd grumble, could be heard to say
That if he went to Heybrook Bay
And never ever made a start
On salvaging in different parts
Then he could only blame himself
For his continued lack of wealth.

And sometimes they would ask him why
He didn't make a change and try
To salvage somewhere else one day?
It might be that, not far away,
Ten tons of brass lay all around
In piles which cried out to be found!
It seemed quite clear; in Heybrook Bay
There wasn't much left anyway.
If they were him, that's what they'd choose.
What had he, anyway, to lose?

He'd thank them for their sound advice
And say politely just how nice
It was that they were so concerned
About how little he now earned.
They might be right, then, to suggest
That hunting elsewhere would be best.
For now, he'd carry on this way
And make no changes to his day.
He'd have his pint, then leave the docks
And search the reefs round Renne's Rocks.

This obstinacy made them mad.
He seemed content with what he had!
Despite their help, he seemed to be
Content to live in poverty.
Well, that was that. They'd had a try.
The bed he'd made was where he'd lie!

Just one or two, though, thought that he
Was not as stupid as he seemed.
Perhaps he had another plan,
One not divulged to any man,
And wasn't seeking brass or lead
But rather something else instead?
Maybe he wasn't after scrap
But rather had a secret map
Which showed him that great treasure lay
Upon the reef near Heybrook Bay?

They'd sometimes tease him, buy him beer
Then sit and chat and bend his ear;
Each day, they'd ask, when leaving port,
Was it only scrap he sought?
He then might look them in the eye
And might, as if to make reply,
Hold their gaze a little while
And gently shake his head ... and smile.

The years went by, and little changed
Though some who noticed thought it strange
That even now, he'd still be found
Out searching that same hunting ground.
With passing years, they all felt sure
He looked no older than before.

Now, over time it's my belief
That fate will always crush the thief;
And you will almost always find
That good will triumph, given time.
The fisherman, though, needed help,
Were he to find, amidst the kelp,
The wreck and chest, if they remained
And if they were to be regained.

HELP ARRIVES

IN spring of nineteen sixty-eight
(I can't recall the exact date)
A doctor bought an old stone barn
Which once housed cattle on a farm.
And there, he planned to spend his life
With his two daughters and his wife.

Edge worked amongst the dreaming spires
Of Oxford, home of gowns and choirs,
Researching what made people tick,
And what went wrong to make them sick.
He loved his work, but secretly
He sought the opportunity
To leave, and start his life anew.
He knew exactly what he'd do;
He'd move the family away
To live in some secluded bay.
The girls would have a beach to comb
With shells to find and bring back home,
While he, the happiest man alive
Would go off every day and dive.

The doctor's wife knew of his plans,
For in the time she'd known this man
He must have surely dived on most
Of all the sites round Britain's coast.

One morning, as they rose from bed,
He glanced towards his wife and said
That they were tired. The children too.
And was a holiday not due?
He'd thought that Plymouth might be good.
They'd walk on Dartmoor, eat good food,
And if in search of things to do…
Perhaps he'd do some diving too?

She laughed. She'd like a holiday,
Enjoy the chance to get away
From work and home tasks for a while
But really! She just had to smile,
For when he told her of the plan
He made it sound as if dry land
Was where he planned, most days, to be
And not, in fact, beneath the sea!

She did, however, briefly pause
To wonder what on earth had caused
Her husband to so suddenly
Propose this trip down to the sea.
He hadn't mentioned it before,
Nor talked of Plymouth, she felt sure.
But never mind. This short break should
Do all of them the world of good.

In fact, her husband didn't dare
To tell her what the true facts were
For fear that she might think him mad
For acting in the way he had.
Last night, he'd not long been in bed
And, tired, was sleeping like the dead
When vividly, he had a dream:
He saw a Plymouth harbour scene.
And in his mind's eye, he could see
A weathered vessel by the quay
And on the deck of salt-stained wood
An ancient fisherman had stood.

And as he dreamed, he felt quite sure
He'd met this sailor long before.
He couldn't match the bearded face
To any recent time or place,
Nor could he summon up a name…
Though was there some strange link with Spain?
The sailor turned without a word
Then smiled, and beckoned him aboard.
The doctor woke and at once knew
Exactly what he had to do:
With haste, he had to make his way
To Plymouth for a holiday.

A few weeks later, they arrived.
That night, they walked through Bretonside
And made their way through cobbled streets
(The ones of which you've heard me speak).
And on the quay they spent some time
Examining a defused mine
Used for collections (now, as then)
To pay for Britain's lifeboat men.

They bought a burger from a stall
Called Cap'n Jasper's – known to all
For serving food and mugs of tea
To all those folk who went to sea.
For centuries the captain's shop
Had been *the* place for crews to stop;
Fresh fragrant flavours there they'd find,
Not weevil-ridden tack and limes.

A little further on, there stood
A boat of burnished salt-stained wood.
The doctor stared, for this boat seemed
Just like the one of which he'd dreamed.
He swore that when the morning came,
And if he then felt just the same,
He'd find the captain of the ship
And ask if he might take a trip.

And here, a pub he recognized;
Its name – the Admiral MacBride.
The doctor felt he knew it well,
Though how, he really couldn't tell,
And asked his wife if she would mind
If he, alone, could spend some time
Inside – enjoy a private beer
And spend a quiet evening here?

Once inside the old oak door,
He glanced across the wooden floor
And froze. For there, to his surprise,
And looking him straight in the eye,
Was sat the fisherman he'd seen
Aboard the boat of which he'd dreamed.
His eyes were bright like burning coals
And seemed to look inside his soul.

A thick black beard lay in a pile
And in its midst, they saw a smile.
With folded sleeves, spread out with care,
His jacket lay down by his chair.
And from the door, a trail of sand
Mixed in with salt led to the man.
Although they never could have met,
For him, it seemed, a place was set.

For round the table were some chairs;
In front of each, a meal prepared.
As if he'd known when Edge would arrive
A foaming just-pulled pint beside.
He stood. "Dear doctor! You've not changed;
How nice it is to meet again.
I can't think how long it must be
Since you and I last put to sea.

"Please, take a seat. You must be tired
After such a lengthy drive.
From here to Oxford, I must say,
Is quite a distance for one day.
The others shouldn't be too long;
In fact, unless I'm very wrong
They'll get here in an hour or so –
They haven't got so far to go."

The doctor sat there, taking stock.
He felt quite faint. Completely shocked.
Although he felt he knew this chap
Relaxing in his captain's cap.
He really hadn't made a plan
To trick his wife and meet this man,
So was this chance? Or, as it seemed,
Had he been summoned in his dreams?

And more. How could this man have known
Where he and Jenny had their home?
He must have sensed when he'd arrive
To get fresh beer put on the side.

And come to that, he felt he knew
Both captain and the barman too
As if some meeting had been set
With people he once might have met…

Outside the Admiral MacBride
A navy man was passing by.
He worked in London, but today
Had travelled down to holiday.
He, like the doctor, didn't know
Quite what had made him want to go.
Perhaps it was a Plymouth scene
Which just last month came in his dream?

In any case, one thing was clear;
He'd get to do some diving here.
He'd tried it once some years before,
But only gone in from the shore.
But now he planned to get afloat
And do some diving from a boat.
He saw the pub. Perhaps he'd find
The skipper of a boat inside?

He wandered in, and there ahead
He saw a table had been set.
Around, a group of people sat –
And one had on a captain's cap.
He made his way towards the group;
The captain, smiling, turned and stood
And called him over. "Take a seat.
So, Hunter, once again we meet!"

The same bemusement filled his head
As that which Doctor Edge had felt.
And which a cook from Kent now shared:
A dream had caused him to prepare
Provisions which he'd carried there
Together with his diving gear;
Kit Adrian had packed away
Unsure it'd yet see light of day.

The three men there each thought it rude
To go, or leave the beer and food
So sat and chatted. Found it strange
That they all knew each other's names.
They had the sort of ease you find
With those who know each other's minds;
In fact, as if they'd somehow known
Each other sometime long ago.

In conversation, it was clear
That something odd had brought them here.
Yet none of them now felt alarmed –
The others clearly meant no harm
And each of them, they all now knew,
Was also trained in diving too,
And each had planned to find a way
To do some in the coming days.

Tomorrow they would have to meet.
At nine, they'd gather in the street
And see if they could find afloat
Some dinghy or some fishing boat
Whose captain might agree to show
The three of them some place to go
Where they might don their kit and try
To get some safe and scenic dives.

Till now, the captain's words were few.
He let them plan what they would do.
But at this point, he stood and spoke:
He was the skipper of a boat
And had it moored not far from here,
All kitted out with diving gear.
Perhaps they'd like to come next day
And dive with him in Heybrook Bay?

The deal was done. What luck they'd had!
You know, this really wasn't bad
To find fine friends, fine beer and food
And now a boat! Yes, this was good!
And, strangely, not a single one
Now seemed to know just how they'd come
To meet each other. No ... not clear
Quite how it was they'd all met here...
The memory of dreams and such ...
Had blown away...
Like so much dust...

DIVING TOGETHER

NEXT day, as arranged, they all met by the quay.
They had not brought their weightbelts or tanks full of air,
For the captain had told them he'd long had things ready,
And once on the boat they'd find everything there.
A new valve to breathe with, and mask, fins and snorkel,
A knife and a wet suit for each, made to fit,
Would be laid out on bunks in the berths he'd prepared
With a clean canvas bag which would hold their new kit.

The sight of the vessel left Hunter disturbed,
For he thought that he knew her from some time before…
How strange he should think this – and how strange as well
That he pictured her moored by some far Spanish shore.
Puzzled, he gazed at her burnished brown timbers
And bow, where he noticed a few peeling words –
Inscribed in old paintwork the words *Arctic Tern*
And beneath them was painted a black and white bird.

The boat leaped with joy as they sailed from the harbour –
And fish, near the bow, skipped on spume 'neath bright skies
As Daisy stood sniffing the sharp salty spray
With her fur blown in great woollen waves from her eyes.
As they sailed out past Bovisand, on to the Shagstone
Old Bruno told how they would gather up scrap;
They'd swim up the line which was towed by the vessel
To put all the pieces they had in a sack.

On reaching the Shagstone, he lowered the anchor;
Attached were three ropes which then drifted behind.
The engines were cut, and they put on their kit.
They pulled down their masks and flopped over the side.
The cool Plymouth waters seeped in through their wet suits
And chilled them as, headfirst, they sank deep below.
They swam to the end of a rope as they drifted
And, searching for scrap, they then swam to and fro.

They had a great time – filled the sack, in one day,
With more scrap than the fisherman ever achieved,
But despite their success and the money it meant,
The captain was not really happy, it seemed.
He said he was pleased with the metal they'd found,
But was saddened their searches had not yet revealed
Any timbers or, maybe, an old rusting anchor –
The signs of a wreck which had long been concealed.

Next day, and the ones for the rest of the week,
Was successful in terms of the metal they found.
But, search as they might through the weeds on the reefs,
They still couldn't see any wreckage around.
At night, they would gather to drink in the pub
And relax, and proclaim how they all were so glad
To have come on this trip, to have met these new friends,
And what excellent diving each day they had had.

A week soon went by with the crew in good spirit.
The captain grew sadder, though, each day they sailed.
It wasn't their fault. How, indeed, could they know
What the future would hold for him if their search failed?
As Saturday's dinner was served in the pub
He decided he had little choice, and that night
He would ask them to stay as he told them a tale
Of a captain they knew, and his desperate plight.

They did as he asked, and when all were replete
He sat forward, then steadily gazed at each one.
They solemnly settled in silence to hear him;
The customers quietened. A tale was to come.
Those standing near by edged in closer to hear him –
A shuffling circle, three deep, round the man.
He'd never before let these people so near.
In this static suspense, he drew breath.
  And began…

"They call it a legend," he said, "and round here
There are many who first heard the tale in their youth.
But like grains of sand in the middle of pearls
You may find in a legend a small grain of truth.
In fact, I assure you, this isn't a legend.
At first, you'll be startled by what you have heard.
Believe me, however – I have inside knowledge –
The story is true, down to every last word.

"Far north, many thousands of years in the past,
A man known as Mad Dog was living a life
Of despicable evil, for no better reason
Than for his enjoyment of pain and of strife.
He looked at the fishermen casting their nets
And he envied their happiness, vowing he'd try
To bring sorrow to all of these men and their folks
And would wipe out their village, which nestled near by.

"He sought out a man who, though simple, was greedy
And found it quite easy to purchase the fool.
In seconds the man had agreed to the deal.
He'd sell out his friends in return for some jewels.
The Mad Dog was happy to watch this betrayal;
His pleasure would surely be well worth the pay.
Indeed, some months later, he stood there and gloated:
All villagers dead, bar the traitor, that day.

"The fisherman knew that his actions were evil,
Was ridden with guilt and decided one day
That he couldn't forgive himself what he had done –
So he set out to drown himself off Wembury Bay.
However, he learned that he still had to live –
This the message he heard from the ghosts of his friends:
A life must be saved; he must save one betrayed,
Then distribute great wealth should he e'er make amends.

"This mission entrusted, the fisherman waited;
For many long years he resided near by
As he awaited his chance to put right his wrongs
And to then find forgiveness, and peacefully die.
Years later, in Spain, he fought once more with Mad Dog;
Saved a life, but then lost all the treasure he'd won.
His friends, though, all swore that they'd come
    back to help him
If ever he called – till his tasks were done.

"As it happened, the victory in Spain was not total.
Although he had managed to save one betrayed
And had gathered great wealth, he had failed at the last:
All the wealth he'd received he'd not given away.
It remained undisturbed – a great mountain of treasure –
He knew where the chest which contained it still lay.
It was out near the Shagstone, just where they'd been diving;
A fortune in silver piled up in the bay.

"I have searched for this treasure for years with no luck.
And it lies where it sank on a boat 'neath the sea.
If I find it, I plan not to keep it at all,
For the man in the tale is a man known to me.
And that fisherman now has grown weary of waiting.
The treasure, once found, will all go to the poor.
He'll at last join the villagers he once betrayed:
Shed his burden of guilt. Rest in peace. Strive no more."

The story was told, and he drew on his ale
As the customers silently walked to the door.
Within a few minutes, they sat there alone –
Just the captain and friends in that pub by the shore.
He slowly stood up, said, "Goodnight, one and all.
Let us now leave for bed. May you sleep well tonight,
For tomorrow we gather at dawn one more time
In our efforts to ease that poor fisherman's plight."

LEAVING PORT

IN the morning, they met on the ancient stone cobbles
Where trawlers still came, and where still you could buy
Cooked fish from a stall which they called Cap'n Jasper's
Though no one around could remember quite why.
From the baker's shop, Jacka's, they bought some crisp loaves
And the four of them noticed how strange all this seemed,
For the smells and the places all seemed quite familiar,
As if they had visited once in a dream.

The doctor leaned out from the bow as they sailed
Staring out at the Shagstone, and trying his best
To look out for a clue (though he didn't know what)
Which might guide him to finding that old treasure chest.
As he looked at the wavetops, he thought that he glimpsed
Some green bird, now and then, in the midst of the swell.
Had he seen it before? He felt sure that he had
Although where this had been, he could no longer tell.

2 The Search for the Spanish Wreck

THE WRECK DISCOVERED

THE boat forged on through ice-blue waters,
The warming sun was climbing now,
And brilliant beams bounced off the drops
Which splintered from the thrusting bow.
She surfed the crests of gentle waves
And joyfully she made her way
Through friendly waters past the point
Then cut a line towards the bay.

And now they came to Renne's Rocks.
Up in the bow, there stood the crew
All looking keenly round about,
Accompanied by Daisy too.
They'd listened hard the night before
To what the captain said to do.
To find the wreck of which they'd heard
They'd search the shore and sea for clues.

The captain cut the engines now.
The Arctic Tern rocked peacefully
With gentle creaking from the decks
Adrift upon a glassy sea.
The sparkling swell, the burning sun,
And squinting at the coast and skies
Caused the surgeon's head to ache
So for a while, he shut his eyes.

From random patterns which appeared
A shape in grey was slowly born.
At first, it swirled like rolling mist,
But gradually it took on form.
A beak appeared. A tiny head
And graceful wings all came in turn.
He'd seen this image on the bow:
This was, he knew, an Arctic tern.

And as he watched, with eyes still shut,
The bird took flight and seemed to soar
Above some ancient Spanish ship.
He'd surely seen all this before?
With that, the bird dissolved again,
The swirling mists went just as fast.
He opened both his eyes again
To see the bird above the mast!

The others also saw it too:
It wheeled before them in the skies
And as the surgeon first had found,
The bird was one they recognized.
The captain stared, then ran at once
To fire the engines, for he knew
They'd find the boat they sought once more
By following where'er she flew.

And as the bird now turned to shore
The boat, her namesake, followed suit.
The captain copied every move
Precisely following her route.
And if she flew ahead too fast,
The crew aboard would quickly find
That she would circle for a while
Ensuring they'd not fall behind.

They tacked and turned for quite some time
And to the fisherman it seemed
She'd lost the wreck – could not recall
Just where the sinking boat had been.
Then suddenly she seemed to pause
And, hovering, let out a cry.
She swooped – then soaring at the sun
Was lost within the burning sky.

The captain knew the wreck was close
And swiftly, now, he marked the spot
By dropping from the stern a buoy
He'd tied onto a weighted shot.
And from the stern, he hung the anchor,
Measured, as they'd done before,
To hang beneath *The Arctic Tern*
Three feet above the ocean's floor.

He called the crew, explained the search.
They'd slowly motor up and down
Until the anchor snagged below;
In this way would the wreck be found.
They took their places quickly now,
And minutes later were prepared.
The winches ready, hands on deck
The wreck, in no time, would be theirs!

He fired the engines up at once
And, gently now, he turned the boat.
He took a bearing on the shore,
As now the bow brushed past the float.
He'd planned to search for many hours
But all at once, the line went taut –
The boat had travelled not two yards
Before her anchor had been caught!

The captain seized the line at once.
The crew, with great excitement, stood
And watched the captain haul it in.
Stuck to the anchor flukes was wood!
He sighed aloud – sank to his knees.
The ancient wreck in Plymouth Sound –
The one for which he'd searched these years –
Had, without doubt, this day been found!

They left the buoy to mark the site
Too late to dive that afternoon.
They scarcely could believe their luck
That they had found the wreck so soon.
The captain, though, was most relieved;
For some, the search had scarce begun.
He'd spent much longer, though, than that:
For him, the search was lifetimes long.

DIVING THE WRECK

AT dawn the next morning they gathered again
And set sail for the wreck which, not one day before,
Had been found by the crew of the old fishing ship
After centuries lying upon the sea floor.
The buoy was still there, in the place where they'd left it
(In fact, if you look from the shore, then you might
Catch a glimpse of it still: those who don't know the story
Assume it marks lobster pots left overnight).

Approaching now, slowly, the anchor once more
Had been hung from the stern till it caught in the wreck.
With their ship now positioned right over their prize,
The divers now busied themselves on the deck.
The captain had asked that the others go first;
Find the wreck, check its age, and then please look around
In an effort to find where the main deck had been
In the hope that the treasure chest might then be found.

They put on their wet suits, their masks, fins and snorkels,
Their bottles of air, and their valves and their gloves.
They dropped overboard, sinking fast through cool waters
And soon left the fishing boat far up above.
The water glowed green in bright sun from the surface,
All noise from the boat was blocked out as they went;
The hiss of sucked air and the gurgle and tinkle
Of bubbles alone could be heard in descent.

In minutes, they'd nearly completed their journey;
The shot line went straight to the anchor, they knew.
The anchor was fixed without doubt in the wreck
Which a shoal of large fish for a while blocked from view.
As they watched, the fish parted. Beneath them, they saw
Through the gloom, a shape forming amidst the green light.
As they sank down towards it, its form became clearer.
They froze as they met an extraordinary sight.

For there on the bottom was sitting a ship.
Not the battered old timbers they'd come to expect,
But a fully rigged vessel. An octopus pennant
And black skull and crossbones still flew from the wreck.
The sails were still hoisted. The cabin door open.
Some charts could be seen on a table inside.
All the fittings were brass, and were shining like new.
The wheel on the deck slowly spun in the tide.

They swam through the rigging, then paused; somewhere close
Came a slow mournful clanging which echoed around.
They followed the noise to the front of the wheel-house;
The ship's old brass bell was the source of the sound.
They turned from the bell and surveyed the main deck
Then, as one, all the divers drew in a sharp breath:
Right there, only yards away – lid tightly padlocked,
And strapped to the deck by old chains – lay a chest.

Finning gently, and carried along by the current,
They swam in a line through the green eerie gloom.
Their fins raised a mass of fine silt from the timbers
Like the dust blown from books in a long-empty room.
At the chest they discovered that both lock and chains
Had not rusted at all, but seemed almost brand new
And the leather which covered the wood glowed so brightly
It had surely been polished by some ghostly crew?

They did not pause long, but laid out all the tools
Which they'd carried in order to work on the wreck.
Using bolt-shears the divers cut links from the chains,
Till at last, with a clank, they slipped down to the deck.
The chest had been freed. With a crowbar they carried
The lock on the front now came under attack;
With the bar through the hoop of the lock, they all heaved.
It creaked for a moment, then gave with a crack.

The divers thought hard about what they should do,
But it wasn't so easy to know what was best.
Should they lift the lid now, and perhaps find the riches?
Or go – let the fisherman open the chest?
Whatever they did, they must make haste about it
And reach their decision before too long;
They'd been down for an age, and must go or risk drowning.
The air in their bottles was almost all gone.

On the surface, the fisherman waited and watched.
They'd been down on the bottom for ever, it seemed.
Had they found some old wreckage? And was it the ship
Which he'd sought every day, and at night filled his dreams?
At last, bubbles boiled on the shiny sea's surface,
Announcing that divers were soon to appear.
They bobbed to the surface, swam up to the side,
And then silently each of them handed him gear.

They hauled themselves out from the water at last,
And proceeded to clear up their kit without word.
The fisherman helped them to tidy it all,
But they said not a word until each piece was stowed.
At last, Hunter faced him, but still he said nothing.
The tension was more than the sailor could stand.
His voice deep and shaking, he asked, "Did you find her?"
The answer: a piece of eight placed in his hand.

OLD ENEMIES

THE sight of the coin made the fisherman weep.
As he did so, he thanked them for all they had done.
He hadn't, though, finished; they couldn't now help him.
Alone he must finish the trail he'd begun.
"My friend," he exclaimed, "you have given me freedom!
I love you, and thank you with all of my heart.
I shall miss you, but know there are things still to do.
We must say our goodbyes, for I soon shall depart.

"So, goodbye then to Hunter, my oldest of friends.
You should not be plain 'Hunter', but really a Lord.
You saved me this day, but some time in the past
It was I who saved you when I dragged you aboard.
And farewell young Adrian. Thank you again.
Though you might not remember our times on the seas,
You have helped me before in my quest to do good
And have always assisted and been true to me.

"Doctor Edge. Like the others, you share in the treasure.
You prove yourself worthy of high praise indeed.
To a king, many years in the past, you showed kindness;
This treasure, in part, was his thanks for those deeds.
The coins which you've brought to the surface are yours.
They will keep you all wealthy for decades to come.
There are few folk I'll miss. They all stand on this deck
And I've said my goodbyes to them all – except one."

He turned to old Daisy, who sat there and whimpered.
They looked at each other. He offered a smile
But she hung her head low, and slinked sadly towards him.
He knelt, took her paw, and then stroked her awhile.
"Farewell then, my friend. We have known one another
For longer than anyone here might believe.
I have loved you more deeply than any companion.
Don't pine when I've gone." He stood up. "I must leave."

With that, he got changed and once more donned his tank.
He paused at the side, took a last look around.
He would miss many things – the old ship and the pub,
And the swell and the spray as he sailed Plymouth Sound.
He took a deep breath, wiped his eyes with his hand,
Fixed his mask in position, and without more delay
Dropped over the side, gripped the line to the anchor.
With a splash of his fins, he was lost 'neath the waves.

Bruno sank through the gloom. He would have to be quick
For the tide had now turned and the current was strong.
The plankton was thick in the water around him,
A thick cloud of green as it floated along.
He sank ever deeper, and though the light dimmed,
He could make out a flag; in the strong current flow
It still billowed as once it had flown in a gale,
And still hung from the top of the mast far below.

Through rigging and sails he continued to sink,
As the sound of the bell (as they'd said) reached his ears.
Its dull eerie clanging grew louder and faster:
A warning to someone, perhaps, who lived here?
With quickening breaths, he swam on past the wheel-house
And up to the deck, where the chest should be found.
He searched the cold waters, then suddenly saw it!
It sat where it had when the ship had gone down.

The shackles and lock which had once strapped it down
Lay destroyed on the deck, where the divers had been.
The lid, though, was down … had the divers not told him
The lid was left *up*? Or had that been a dream?
A cold shudder seized him. He wasn't alone.
He felt sure something evil was lurking near by.
He anxiously glanced all around, seeing nothing
Then, eyes wide with horror, let out a short cry.

The lid on the chest had begun to creak open.
No hand could be seen to be doing this task
Yet it steadily rose, as coins spilled from the top
And then spun to the deck from the edge of the cask.
The treasures within were as he remembered,
With pieces of eight, by the thousand, inside:
Ten million pounds' worth of old Spanish coins
Now exposed, after hundreds of years, to the tide.

The lid now was up, yet he still couldn't tell
What had caused it to happen. He thought that, maybe,
It was merely the rush of the tide that had done it,
Or just a strong eddy, or swell from the sea?
But deep down he knew that it wasn't that simple.
An enemy lurked there – and one he must beat –
Who had stayed with the ship for these hundreds of years
And who'd waited that time to avenge his defeat.

The fisherman patiently studied the trunk
Till at last from around it, and just as he'd feared,
A flicker of movement was glimpsed at each corner
And then, as he watched, some red flesh appeared.
Eight tentacles writhed round the chest as the body,
All slimy and heaving and pulsing in size,
Sat amidst all the treasure, then turned round to face him:
An octopus glaring with fiery red eyes.

"We meet once again," thought the fisherman slowly,
"And still you are trying to get in my way!
I'd rather not fight, but will happily do so
In order that good shall beat evil this day.
I promised to right all my wrongs, and have done so
Except for one task which you know I have left:
I promised to seek out and win a great fortune
And give it away, so that I can find rest."

He looked to his side, and reached down to his calf.
From a sheath which was strapped there, he pulled out a knife.
He gazed at the creature, now fixed with his stare:
"Get out of my way, if you value your life!"
The octopus, though, didn't move from the chest,
And its tentacles writhed and its red body glowed.
It was set on defending the chest to the last,
And drew strength from the fury the fisherman showed.

The diver went forward. His mind was made up.
He would kill the vile creature! The treasure was his!
Then all of a sudden, he thought of his friends
As they sailed their twelve boats through that strange ocean mist.
In those thousands of years, had he really not learned
That no peace ever lasted if won in a fight?
That no act born of hate or of violence brought good?
That the noblest of aims never made a wrong right?

With that he looked down at the knife that he held.
Many years in the past, he'd had blood on these hands
As betrayal had led to the death of his friends
For a handful of jewels which were cast on the sand.
He let the knife drop. As he did so he sensed
That the creature was fearful to see him let go:
A man armed with hate and a knife may be dangerous;
A man armed with honour's a deadlier foe.

The fisherman slowly swam up to the chest.
He would claim what was his, and would set himself free.
He still had his promise to give to the poor
And he'd keep it.
He knew.
This was his destiny...

RESOLUTION

ABOVE, on the surface, they'd watched as the captain
Had put on his gear and said his goodbyes;
As he'd paused at the side, as his eyes scanned the sea,
As he took one last look at the bright Plymouth skies.
They were puzzled, but watched as he ducked through the waves.
They had not understood what he'd meant – "I must go" –
But had followed the trail of the fine fizzing bubbles
Which had plotted the path that he took down below.

The bubbles had followed the fall of the shot line,
Then moved to the right as he followed the deck.
They paused for a moment – he must have now stopped
At the eerie dull clang of the bell on the wreck.
He set off again, and they thought of him making
His way past the wheel-house, and past the bell too.
Then they saw that the bubbles had once again stopped
And they knew he'd have paused when the chest was in view.

It was then that his actions seemed hard to explain,
For the path of the bubbles now didn't move on.
Was he caught in net? Had he run into trouble?
Just why was he sitting there? What had gone wrong?
Their worry increased, till at last they decided
To send down a diver to come to his aid.
As they made preparations, he set off again.
The final approach to the chest had been made.

They stood there in silence – then Hunter glanced up.
In the distance, he'd noticed the cry of a bird.
It was mournful and plaintive, and caught in the breeze,
Grew increasingly loud, until all the friends heard.
The call was unlike any other they knew,
So they turned, scanned the waves, and then shielding their eyes
They looked to the sun and the brightly lit clouds
Where the Arctic tern, high above, soared through the skies.

It came out of the sun, with its smooth agile wings
Flicking this way and that as they caught on the breeze.
It banked and it swooped, and then levelled its flight
Till it surfed through the spray which whipped up from the sea.
Approaching their boat, it gained height once again
And then banked round the mast as it circled the deck
With its eyes fixed below – not on them, but the bubbles
Which rose in a stream from the site of the wreck.

The bird was the same one which, not long before,
Had appeared and had led them to where the wreck lay.
But why had the bird, with its mission accomplished,
Come back to this place so late on in the day?
A sudden sharp wind gusted hard at the ship
And from nowhere, dark clouds rose to blot out the sun.
A sense of foreboding surrounded the crew.
The bird was the herald of bad things to come…

Below, in the chest, the red octopus glowered
As four of its tentacles gripped the chest tight.
The other four rippled and writhed near the edge
Reaching out for the fisherman, ready to fight.
The diving knife, dropped by the fisherman, sparkled;
It had spun like speared fish as it spiralled to deck.
With both his hands empty, the fisherman came
Kicking silt, as he swam, from the planks of the wreck.

He reached for the treasure – was suddenly seized
By a tentacle; first just by one, then by more.
He tried to pull back, but another coiled round him;
His arm was soon gripped by not three, but all four!
The tip of a tentacle inched round his neck
And its tightening grip made him dizzy with pain.
He tried with his fingers to prise the thing off
But the strength of the suckers meant all was in vain.

Two tentacles, soon, had been squeezed round his neck
And were hauling his head ever closer. In fright
He looked up at the octopus – saw its head tilted:
Its sharp evil beak had been opened to bite!
He wedged both his knees on the side of the chest
But the strength of the creature was more than a match.
The octopus seemed to be reeling him in:
He wasn't a fisherman now, but the catch!

His head was just inches away from its jaws
When he reached, with the arm he'd kept free, to his belt.
His head was engulfed by the octopus limbs,
And he couldn't look down at the pouch which he felt.
The octopus sensed sudden danger – in fear
It reached for the arm, thus releasing its grip.
The fisherman rolled back in fresh clouds of silt
Pushing hard with his feet as the creature let slip.

He rapidly opened the pouch on his belt,
And his fingers took hold of the contents within.
He pulled out his hand, with the fingers clenched tight,
As the octopus pushed off and started to swim.
One pulse with its limbs, and it shot fast ahead –
Like a deadly torpedo it sped at the man.
The fisherman waited until the last moment
Then lunged and released what he held from his hand.

The thing that he threw was a glittering jewel.
Betrayal had long ago paid for this gem.
'Twas the last of the treasure he'd once had as payment:
A ruby as red as the blood of his friends.
"You once gave me this," thought the captain, "and now
It becomes my defence in this time of attack.
The burden of guilt which came with it remains.
It's that burden I hurl at you! Here, have it back!

The octopus, struck, stopped at once in its flight
Sinking down to the deck, trailing limbs as if dead.
The blow of the guilt struck as hard as a hammer:
It suddenly knew where its actions had led.
It felt the distress which the villagers felt.
It could feel all the pain, knew the Spaniards' tears.
Far worse, though, the terrible anguish and unrest
Which the fisherman had borne for two thousand years.

A fizzing of bubbles rose up round its body
Consumed by the conflict of guilt, hate and love.
The water around boiled and belched bursting bubbles
Which soared to the sea's shining surface above.
The fisherman watched this with deepening sadness.
The centuries had taught him one thing through and through:
No matter their actions, you shouldn't hate the *men*
Though you might hate their motives, and what they might *do*.

He swam to the chest, seized a handful of coins,
Watched them trickle and spin to the decking below;
A secret supply for the poor and the sick
Of which all local people would very soon know.
He'd long since made plans for the way they'd be given;
The needy, at night, would abandon their pride
And would pin a note pleading their case for some silver
Upon the oak door of the old pub, MacBride.

The crew on the boat far above were still waiting;
They'd watched as the bubbles had moved to the chest.
They'd waited an age … then the bubbles moved back
Where the column moved slightly, and then came to rest.
But now, as they watched, they were panicked indeed,
For a turbulent torrent of fizzing appeared:
The sea spat with anger, like boiling-hot fat;
The furious frenzy showered salt spray, and fear…

A minute or two, and the maelstrom subsided.
The sea, once again, settled down, became calm.
They ought to have felt great relief at this sight
But the stillness they saw filled them all with alarm.
There weren't any bubbles to show their friend breathed.
Some feathers which floated alone marked the place.
They looked, but the Arctic tern too now seemed gone:
Of the bird, and their friend, they could see not a trace.

The silence now hung like a damp rug around them.
They stepped in bewilderment back from the side.

They had not been distracted for more than a minute.

But in those few moments, though …

Daisy had died.

RELEASE

NOW, to Hunter it seemed that the death of old Daisy
Could not be coincidence. She'd not have gone
Had she not known her master was leaving for good…
The fisherman! No, he'd been down far too long!
In seconds, he'd climbed to the top of the cabin,
Was frantically scanning the sea all around:
The fisherman might not have come to the surface,
But, surely, some sign of him would yet be found?

He strained in the glare of the sun as it settled,
A bright orange ball quenched in sea off Rame Head.
There was no sign of life, not a ripple in sight
And he knew, in his bones, that their friend must be dead.
Nonetheless, they must hunt for him, lest he be trapped
In the rigging and sails, or perhaps in the nets
Which had snagged on the timbers and been left behind
And now hung like a shroud from the sides of the wreck.

He ordered his colleagues to ready themselves
And told them which tools they should each bring along.
A knife for the netting. A spare air supply.
A torch, for the sun had now very near gone.
With daylight receding, they dropped from the boat,
And together descended the shot line they'd laid.
Their torch beam struck down through the quickening gloom
As above, fading sunlight washed warm on the waves.

They descended with speed, for they knew the way well –
Yet the ship, when they reached her, was not as before.
Bright timbers were rotten. The sails were all holed.
Now no clang of a bell, but the creak of a door
As it swung from one hinge from a barnacled cabin.
A mass of thick weed trailed like hair from the mast.
They could see her grow old right in front of their eyes
As if they were watching as centuries passed.

A creak and a groan, and the mast slowly toppled
And fell to one side in a cloud of grey silt.
The wreck, so it seemed, was collapsing around them.
The decks had already developed a tilt.
There wasn't a moment to waste! Hunter swam
Past the wheel-house and bell till he came to the place
Where the chest had once sat, but the light from his torch
Showed him nothing. Of treasure, there wasn't a trace.

In the shadows near by, though, his torch beam struck steel
And he swam quickly onwards to see what was there;
The fisherman's weight belt, his knife and his valve
Were laid out by his bottle, now empty of air.
He never had left a bottle unfinished
And other things, too, he had done in his way:
For there, with the sleeves neatly folded across it,
The fisherman's jacket, they noticed, now lay.

Their own air supply had now fallen so low
That they knew they should surface at once if they could.
They couldn't delay any longer, and turned
And swam swiftly through tangles of fast-rotting wood.
They searched for the spot where the shot line had been,
And then found the right place – yes, of that they were sure –
But the shot line was no longer there to be found
And the anchor had gone from the rocky sea floor.

They panicked, and headed at once for the top
Swimming up in the welter of bubbles they'd made.
They burst into air, ripped their masks from their heads,
Spat their valves from their mouths, ditched their tanks to the waves.
And the boat which they'd dived from was no longer there!
She had sailed, so it seemed, on her own out to sea
Having pulled up her anchor, and started her engines –
But that, they all knew, couldn't possibly be…

Nonetheless, as the sun yielded gently to moonlight
And Hunter was wiping salt spray from his eyes
He thought that perhaps he could see, silhouetted,
The shape of a boat as it crossed the dark skies.
And he'd swear that he made out a treasure chest's shape,
With a man in the bow, and that there by his side
Was a dog looking happily up at her master
United once more on the wind and the tide.

If it hadn't been dark and they hadn't now started
To swim as a group for the silvery shore,
He might then have seen that the ship had been joined
By some friends who were sailing a dozen ships more…

The crew and their wives woke next day to the feeling
That something around them was not as it seemed.
They'd slept like the dead, but strange visions of treasure
And a captain called Bruno had passed through their dreams.
Not one of them now could remember the time
That they'd spent on the ship in those last seven days,
For their memories all were erased by the dawn
Like a mist which dispersed in the sun's warming rays.

They packed with the thought that they'd merely been tourists.
With that in their minds, they all made their way home
With no memory now of the friends they had made
And convinced that they'd spent all their time on their own.
Steve Hunter gained rank, and was soon made a sea lord
And happily lived with his good wife, Louise.
He never once thought of a different career
As an admiral sailing the world's stormy seas…

Up near Oxford, Chris Edge and his lovely wife Jenny
With young Alexandra, Victoria too,
Lived happily – he with his medical work,
And she with her silversmith's work still to do.
She also made brooches – she didn't know why –
Showing faces of friends, and with these they seemed pleased.
And Edge never thought of a time long ago
When he'd saved a king's life in a land overseas.

As for Adrian … well … that's a mystery still.
It might never be clear what he knew then (or knows)
For with Bridget his wife, and their sons Jack and Patrick,
He moved back to Plymouth not that long ago.
Arriving, he found himself work in a pub
And of their new barman the locals all swore
That he took to the job in the old pub MacBride
In a way that suggested he'd done it before…

THREE TALES

SO now I've finished. You have heard
Three separate stories. One occurred
In northern parts: an evil man
Set out to conquer other lands.
A local village was betrayed
By some poor fisherman he paid
To sell his friends. All of them died
And only this one man survived.

The second tale was set in Spain.
I won't repeat it all again,
For you will know how Bruno went
To seek a peaceful settlement
With Spain, and how he saved the king
From certain death from poisoning,
And how the traitor's boat was lost
In Heybrook Bay, near Renne's Rocks.

The final tale, as now you know,
Was set some thirty years ago.
The traitor's boat was found once more
Upon the rocky ocean floor
Unchanged by all the centuries
She'd spent beneath the Devon seas.
The treasure still lay on the ship.
An octopus was guarding it.

But what connects these times of old?
And what connects the tales I've told?
Foul betrayal, certainly
Occurs in two tales of the three.
But could it be that evil deeds
Can never in the end succeed
And, for this reason, we will find
All wrongs are righted, given time?

So, was the man in northern climes
Who sailed the seas in olden times
And took the jewels and sold his friends,
The same man who then made amends
For all his selfishness and greed,
By helping in his hour of need
Lord Hunter, who might yet have drowned
Unless (by chance?) he'd first been found?

And was he, by Lord Hunter, asked
To sail with him to foreign parts?
And did he then proceed to save
The Spanish king, who'd been betrayed?
And was this man the same as he
Who later went beneath the sea
And made a living raising scrap
By diving down with ropes and sacks?

And did he sail through centuries
On northern and on local seas
In just one boat? Did he arrive
In waters down near Bretonside
Aboard the good ship *Arctic Tern*?
Was this the same boat which you learned
Was sailed to Spain, and from whose decks
The divers later sought the wreck?

And was that howling hairy man
Who'd also lived in northern lands,
For whom plain evil was the goal
(Who bought, in jewels, the very soul
Of that poor man aboard his boat
And paid him to betray his folk),
And Mad Dog Morgan one and the same?
Did he betray the king of Spain?

And finally, you must decide
If all the divers I've described
(Like Doctor Edge and Adrian
And Hunter) were the self-same men
Who sailed with Bruno first to Spain:
And did they really come again
When, lifetimes later, Bruno asked
His friends to help him in his task?

Perhaps the debts are fully paid
And Bruno saved a man betrayed
– A token act to make amends
In part for having killed his friends.
And having caused great pain before,
Perhaps he tried to aid the poor
And help those folk of failing health
By giving them enormous wealth
Which, with his friends, he later found
Upon that wreck in Plymouth Sound.

TODAY

SO now you've listened to my tale
Of Bruno, and of how he sailed
With friends aboard *The Arctic Tern*;
I hope you'll treasure what you've learned.
And one day you might think of it
And go to Plymouth, see the ships
And all the places I've described:
The pub, the Admiral MacBride,
The drinking trough and Wembury beach
And Heybrook Bay are all in reach,
And other sites are close at hand
Like Cap'n Jasper's burger stand.

You might then go to Wembury beach;
When tide is low you there might seek
The jewels the fisherman threw down
Where waves roll in from Plymouth Sound.
Occasionally, a searching hand
Which gently sifts the seashore sand
Will find some item thought to be
No more than glass washed by the sea.
Such coloured pieces (red and green)
May not in fact be what they seem
And may in fact be something more
Than broken bottle on the shore.

At Heybrook Bay one sometimes spots
Some wooden fragments on the rocks.
Amongst them, some old bits are found
Whose weathered surfaces are browned
And worn and ragged. Parts like these
Have surfaced from beneath the seas
From wrecks long lost, and some may float
Towards the shore from Mad Dog's boat
Which lies not very far at all
From Renne's Rocks, you will recall.

At night-time, you might also hear
A dog that barks. Well, never fear:
They say that Daisy walks around
At nightfall in the darkened town
As she revisits all the sites
That she remembers, and by night
Will make her way towards the docks,
Or walk the shore near Renne's Rocks.
If at the Barbican one day
You catch a glimpse of some poor stray,
Then show some kindness to the hound –
It might be Daisy that you've found.

THE END

Acknowledgements

*I should like to thank the crew — whether volunteer
or press-ganged. Thanks to Bruno, Clare McClintock,
Seana Smith, and to Margaret Rule and the
Mary Rose Diving Team, for many happy memories
of diving days; to Clare Dollery, who became an
ill-tempered parrot; and to the Hunter, Edge, Gardner
and Naunton-Morgan families; to Nick Poullis,
Mónica Bratt and Miriam Richardson for believing
when others had less faith. To all at Walker Books,
who had similar passion, commitment and
professionalism and were prepared to "take the chance".
Especial thanks to Mary, who was widowed by this book
and without whom it would never have been written,
and to Andrew Gardner, whom I miss very much.
He represented honesty and the best of journalism.*

*Finally, if there are noble views espoused in this book,
these belong to my parents. They have devoted their lives
to their children, and to the children of others.
My love and respect to them.*